"Do you love me, Cathy? Real love, not just friendship?"

She nodded. "Real love. Right from the start."

"Darling!" Caught up in his arms, she surrendered to his kisses. Everything was forgotten except the mutual ecstasy that transcended every other thought.

"I'll never let you go, never!" he declared, at last.

But Cathy drew away. "Neil, what are we thinking of? We mustn't give in to what we feel. Everything is against it."

He kissed her again, intensely. "There's nothing against it, nothing! I love you and you love me, that's all that matters."

Sadly, she shook her head. "No, Neil. There is a gap between us that cannot be bridged— not now, not even by the power of our love."

The Aston Hall Romance Series:

Mary Faid

NO STARS
SO BRIGHT

PINNACLE BOOKS   LOS ANGELES

NO STARS SO BRIGHT

An original Pinnacle Books edition, published by special arrangement with Aston Hall Publications, Inc.

First printing, October 1980

ISBN: 0-523-41120-0

Printed in the United States of America

PINNACLE BOOKS, INC.
2029 Century Park East
Los Angeles, California 90067

CHAPTER ONE

THE LIGHTS WERE going up in the Square as Neil Drummond stepped from the station taxi on a bleak January afternoon.

"Home again, Mr. Neil!" The driver's rubicund face wore a large grin. It was an encouraging sight for the newly returned exile.

"Home again," he echoed. "So you haven't forgotten me, Tom. It's been five years."

"Ay, it will be that, right enough. Your folks will be pleased to see you! I heard your father was ill. The whole town's sorry."

Tom was exaggerating, of course. Nethershaw was expanding, and many of its citizens did not know his father. Still, with the older folk the name of Drummond was one to conjure with. This very Square had been called after Neil's great-great grandfather, who was largely responsible for building it; and the family firm had been active ever since.

When Tom Bain had driven away, the young man took time, before climbing the short flight of steps to the big gray house, which dominated the scene, to stand and look about him.

Drummond Square was still as he remembered it but with some noticeable differences. Buildings like the Church, the Bank, and the row of offices with apartments above had not altered. Neither had the central gardens with the memorial fountain. But there were changes on the south side.

The row of crumbling cottages had been cleared away to give place to a smart new building which must be the new Medical Center he'd heard about. A modern apartment building looked slightly garish in the gathering dusk: it would not last so long as the old cottages! Then there were the shops.

Some of these had new fronts of gleaming plate glass; others had disappeared altogether. He was pleased to note, however, that Jessie Paterson's little newspaper and sundries shop was still intact, the light in the window beaming steadily. Jessie had been there in her tiny shop all his life; the Square would not be the same without her.

As he watched, more and more lights appeared in the windows, seeming to welcome him back. "No stars so bright as the lights of home," ran his thoughts as he turned to mount the steps of Airlie House, not sure of what he was going to find there, for he had not notified his family of the exact time of his arrival.

At the top of the steps he halted again, aware that once that door was opened he would be stepping back from an independent existence into an old, inhibiting routine.

Yet he was not altogether unwilling. After five years of testing himself in new surroundings, he had acquired a confidence in life and in his own abilities. No longer was he the raw, twenty-three-year-old who had rushed off from his home town, broken-hearted, vowing never to return.

Gripping the brass bell socketed in the stonework, he gave it a decisive pull and stood waiting. There was a light in the nearest window and in the one above—his grandmother's room—and in a moment the hall was lighted as well and the door was opened, hesitantly at first, then with a will. Before him stood a plump, middle-aged woman, her comely face wreathed in smiles.

"Hello, Susan, it's me!"

"Ay, it's you, Mr. Neil. Well, well, we didn't expect—My, but it's good to see you!"

He took the extended hand, squeezed it, and impulsively placed a kiss on the rosy cheek.

"Good to see you, too, Susan!" As they gazed at each other, he saw moisture in her eyes. His own were moist, too. Susan Brodie had come to Airlie House as nursemaid when he was born. Now in her fifties, she was still here as housekeeper, trusted and faithful.

"How is my father?" he asked, setting down his case in the spacious hall with its indefinable air of departed splendor.

"He's on the mend. He'll be all right, now that you're home."

Was he to believe her? "A slight stroke," was how his mother had described the sudden illness in her letter. He was on no account to hurry home as his father was already recovering, but in the near future, perhaps, he could return for a visit.

Between the lines he had sensed acute anxiety. It was all that was needed to bring him to a decision. Five years ago, after obtaining a science degree in marine biology, he had been only too glad to accept the offer of a junior lectureship in a California university.

The new life among total strangers, with the fascination of the work he loved, had turned his mind outward, leaving no time to brood on the blow that Celia Carr had dealt him. Though the hurt remained, deep down, he had learned to hide it.

He had felt so far cured indeed, that he had actually contemplated returning home even before the word came about his father. It coincided with an opening in a Strathclyde college which matched the post he was in, lecturing and doing research work at Loch Creenan, a few miles from Nethershaw.

So here he was, ready to adjust himself again to home life and to help his parents in their time of stress. He owed them that. They had financed and encouraged him in his studies, in spite of the fact that his father had once expected him to take over the family business. They had even understood his need to get away from everything that would remind him of his broken engagement.

"Your father and mother are in there." Susan nodded toward the door of what was still called the sitting room. A stately drawing room, also bedrooms and nursery occupied the upper story, with chilly attic rooms above.

There was also a semi-basement, originally

the servants' quarters but now unoccupied, as Susan, the only resident help, had a room on the ground floor. It was a house for a large family of means, not for people growing old in times of inflation.

Having hung up his coat, Neil slowly opened the sitting room door, marking the occupants before they became aware of his presence. There they were, one on either side of the black marble fireplace in which a coal fire flickered. His mother wore a wrap round her shoulders and, though her face was still sweet and young looking, her hair showed streaks of white.

The sight of his father gave him a shock, he was so gray and drawn, as if life held no more savor for him. But as Neil advanced into the room, there was a dramatic change. Light sprang into the sunken eyes as he attempted to rise from his chair.

"Neil, my boy. Home at last!" His voice came haltingly, but there was no doubt about his joy at seeing his son.

With an arm round his shoulder, Neil settled him back in his chair.

"Yes, I'm home. How are you feeling, Dad?"

"I'm fine, just fine." His voice lacked conviction, however. The young man looked at his mother for confirmation. Evelyn Drummond smiled shakily, her face flushed with emotion.

"He's certainly improving, Neil."

"Good!" Embracing her warmly, he kissed the trembling lips. "You must let me help you both. That's what I came home for."

"We've been living for the day, Neil. What kind of journey had you?"

"Very smooth. Plane to Prestwick, airline bus to Glasgow. Then the train and Tom Bain's taxi. Tom hasn't changed, though some other things have."

His father inquired shakily—"for the better, don't you think?"

"Well, it was time those old cottages were down, and it must be convenient to have the Medical Center so near. You've done a good job there, Dad."

"Ay." Then, bitterly—"I'd planned to do more, when this happened. It's terrible to be so helpless!"

Neil said encouragingly—"Cheer up, Dad! If I know you, you'll soon be up and doing."

At that moment, Susan Brodie appeared at the door.

"Would you like something to eat just now, Mr. Neil?"

His mother glanced at the clock. "It's not too early for tea, I think. We'll have it in here as usual, Susan. It's fish, Neil. Your father is on a light diet. Is that all right?"

"Of course. Any chance of chips?" he inquired, with a grin at the housekeeper.

She beamed at him. "Sure, there is. I mind how you used to love them."

When she left, he helped his mother pull out the gate-leg table and lay the cloth.

"We seldom use the diningroom now," she explained. "Heating is so expensive these days!"

"You ought to have central heating, Mom.

Everybody has it where I've come from."

She smiled wistfully. "We put off too long and now we can't afford it."

So things were not going too well financially, as he had suspected. Before he had time to reply, there was a knock on the ceiling above them. A summons to be obeyed.

His mother smiled. "That's Grandmamma. She must have heard you."

"Yes, I'd better go up. How is she these days?"

"Wonderful, apart from some arthritis. She still comes downstairs for meals. Will you tell her tea's nearly ready, Neil?"

He ran upstairs two at a time, just as he used to do, the years of absence dissolving as in a dream. Tapping at the well-remembered door, he walked into his grandmother's domain.

Though the room was spacious, it had a crowded look, for in it were packed all her personal belongings and cherished items of furniture. As a boy he had loved to explore these drawers and cupboards. One had to get permission, of course, which wasn't always given, for Grandmamma was an unpredictable old lady. When you expected severity, you often got kindness, and the opposite also applied.

Strong-featured and outspoken, Esther Drummond was respected if not exactly loved by the people of Nethershaw. Fifty odd years ago she had come to Airlie House as a bride, remaining there after her husband died and her son took over. Some maintained she was still the ruler of the household.

On setting eyes on her this evening, erect in her straight-backed chair, knitting needles in hand, Neil was reminded of their native thistle— "You daurna meddle wi' me."

Peering over her spectacles—"So you're home," she observed matter-of-factly. "About time, too."

He had learned to take her blunt manner good-humoredly and bent down to kiss her.

"I hadn't reckoned on coming home just yet, but Dad's illness decided me."

"Well, now you're here, you can sit down and tell me all about yourself."

An interrogation already, trust Gran.

"But tea's nearly ready," he demurred.

"It can wait." There was nothing for it but to take a chair.

"What do you think of your father?" was the first inquiry.

"He looks pretty ill, but I'm told he's getting better."

"Ay, till the next time. Work and worry, that's what did it. All those demolitions and renovations. And to be thwarted by that woman was the last straw."

"What woman was that, Gran?"

"Jessie Paterson, of course. You saw the changes in the Square. He wanted to buy her shop and modernize it, but she wouldn't sell. She's a thrawn one, Jessie."

Neil was thoughtful. "I can see her point of view. It's her home as well, isn't it?"

"Yes," she conceded, "she lives in the flat above. Got a niece staying with her just now who works in that new-fangled Medical Center."

He laughed, "New-fangled, perhaps, but surely a great benefit."

"I don't know," she sighed. "One seldom sees one's own doctor. The old way suited me best. There's too many changes, Neil, and I can't keep up with them. As for your father, he should have eased off long ago. He bit off more than he could chew. Affairs in a muddle, now. God knows what's to become of us."

"Oh, come, it's not like you to be gloomy! Now, let me help you downstairs."

But she was not ready yet. "Bide a wee." She scanned his face with a searching eye. "You look a lot older. I hope you've got over that old love affair?"

He did not pretend to misunderstand. "Long ago. Celia Carr is nothing to me now."

"I'm glad to hear it. Did you know she was back in Nethershaw?"

"No," was the short reply. "With her husband, I suppose."

"Not at all. Celia never married the man she jilted you for. Did nobody ever tell you? She went away for a time and now she's back with her parents, living on them. Now you can hand me my stick, Neil. It's on the floor."

He found the silver-topped cane and gave it to her. Clinging to his arm as they moved to the door, she added some warning advice. "Take care, Neil! Keep out of that girl's way!"

He replied lightly—"Still giving orders, Gran? Thanks for the warning, but it's not needed."

All the same, the news was strangely disturbing. In a sudden flash there rose before him the vivid, tantalizing face of the girl he had been in love with. Then, deliberately thrusting it aside, he proceeded to help his grandmother downstairs.

Jessie Paterson's fingers were freezing, and the tip of her nose was cold and pink as she handled the newly-arrived bundles of papers next morning.

The cold did not bother her, however. Hadn't she risen at the same unearthly hour, winter and summer, for nearly forty years? Even when Matthew, her husband, was alive, she had come down from the flat above to help him with the morning rush.

In her sixties now, Jessie had never been a beauty. She was too thin and pale, her nose a distressing feature, and even the Beautician's across the road could do nothing with her hair. After one trial she had given them up. It wasn't worth the money. Only Cathy Paton, her niece, could make any sort of improvement, and she did it for nothing.

This morning, the rush started as soon as Jessie opened the shop door. Businessmen on their way to the city by train or car snatched up their papers and darted off again. On good terms with them all, Jessie always had the right paper ready. Most of them she had known since their boyhood. Never was a place so bustlingly cheerful as Jessie's shop, even in the dark days of winter.

After early train time, there came a lull,

during which she took time to tidy the counter and sweep up. Upstairs she could hear her niece on the move. Cathy always got up singing. She had a sweet, high voice and sang as if she enjoyed life to the full. This morning it was "Mairi's Wedding."

"Step we gaily, on we go, heel for heel and toe for toe!" Such a rollicking tune, it was all you could do to keep from dancing yourself.

It said a lot for Cathy that she could be so bright after the bad time she'd experienced before coming to Nethershaw. That stepmother of hers had come between her and her father with sorry consequences.

Jessie shook out the doormat with a violence that betrayed her feelings. Her brother Hugh— stupid man!—had had no need to marry again. Cathy, who adored him, was a fine little house-keeper; but if he did have to take a wife, why hadn't he chosen someone who would befriend his only daughter?

The new wife had managed to monopolize him and alienate Cathy at one fell swoop. Though the girl had done her best to adjust, the situation had become unbearable. Well, vowed Jessie, if Cathy had lacked love at home, she was going to get it here with none of the jealousy and back-biting that had made her so miserable.

" 'Step we gaily, on we go—' " She was coming downstairs now, still singing.

"Morning, Aunt Jessie!" Her smiling face and sunny hair irradiated the dull little shop. There was a shining quality about Cathy that emanated, Jessie was sure, from the generous spirit within.

"There you are, Cathy. You could have had another half-hour in bed, you know."

"Not me! I've had my breakfast, Auntie. You nip up and get yours. I'll look after the shop."

"Well, for a wee while. The rush is past."

Alone, Cathy attended to business, thinking what a dear Aunt Jessie was. It was she who had encouraged her to come to Nethershaw and apply for the receptionist job at the Medical Center. It had been a wrench leaving the Highland village where her father was doctor, but her presence there was only a bone of contention.

She was beginning to love her work at the Center, and helping in the shop was fun, a good way of getting to know people.

When her aunt returned, it was nearly time for her to leave.

"Would you like me to hand in the Drummonds' paper on the way?" she asked.

"Oh, I expect Susan Brodie will call for it."

"Yes, but you know how busy she is, with Mr. Drummond ill." It was like Cathy to be thoughtful, young as she was. Jessie did not usually deliver papers, but in a case of illness or old age she made an exception, often using her dinner hour to do so. Since Cathy came, however, there was no need, she was so willing to help out.

"Oh well, perhaps you'd better take it. I daresay that poor man will be glad to get his paper early."

Folding the paper neatly, Cathy observed—

"You're an angel, Auntie, being sorry for Mr. Drummond after the way he treated you, threatening you with all sorts of things if you didn't sell the shop to him."

"I'm no angel," she returned dryly. "He got as good as he gave. I'd right on my side; he couldn't force me. Mind you," she went on, "Andrew Drummond's not a bad sort, just that he can't see anyone stand in his way. He's like his own mother, that way. She's a proper madam! Andrew's wife is a gentle sort of body, can't stand up to her."

"Isn't there a son?" asked Cathy.

"Ay, Mr. Neil. He's expected home soon from America. Been away for five years. He went away with the Brain Drain."

Her niece chuckled. "Is he very brainy?"

"So they say. He's a lecturer. Something to do with fish."

"It sounds a very damp occupation," commented Cathy as she prepared to step out into the cold morning air.

The gardens in the Square looked quite pretty in the pale light, the bushes sparkling with frost. Even the memorial fountain dedicated to a former "Neil Drummond, Provost of this town" was handsome in a Victorian sort of way. Was he, too, interested in fish? The present Neil was probably a cold sort of man, more taken up with his calling than with mere human beings. Scientists were like that.

The steps of Airlie House were treacherous with ice. There was a hand rail on either side, but Cathy went marching up regardless, only to skid on the top step and come down with a crash. Some bottles of milk that were standing there crashed too, and a white cascade poured down the steps.

Benumbed, she just sat there, viewing the disaster. Then the door opened and a man looked out. He was very tall—especially from her present position!—and his dark eyes surveyed her with some concern.

Struggling to her feet with his assistance, she gasped—

"I'm sorry! I've spilled all your milk."

"We'll get more, don't worry. I hope you're not hurt?"

"Not really. Bruises, I expect." Her knees were smarting. Goodbye to that new pair of tights!

Neil had been passing the door when he heard the crash. Whatever he had expected to see, it wasn't the flushed face and apologetic blue eyes of this pretty girl. He picked up the sodden newspaper.

"Sorry again," said Cathy. "If you dry it, I think you'll be able to read it! It's from Miss Paterson."

Light dawned. "I see. Thank you for bringing it. Are you the niece that lives with her?"

"I can't think how you know."

A smile lit up his rather somber face. "My grandmother mentioned it."

"Then you must be Mr. Neil, home from America. I've heard about you, too." Aunt Jessie hadn't hinted how nice he was, in spite of his interest in fish. She went on—"If you would fetch a cloth or something, I'll wipe the step before the milk freezes."

He went inside to bring back what was needed, insisting on doing the job himself. As he knelt there, she remarked:

"It's not quite right, a man like you doing this."

He got to his feet grinning. "How do you know what I'm like?"

"Well, I heard you were very brainy. You lecture people."

He laughed. "That's only a part of me. As your job is only a part of you, no doubt. You work in the Medical Center, don't you?"

"I'm a receptionist there. I start at half-past eight, so I'd better go. Sorry about the milk."

"And I'm sorry you fell. So long, then!"

Cathy looked back to wave to him. He was still there on the step looking after her. In spite of the chilly air, she felt a warmth running through her. Now she had made another friend in Nethershaw. She needed friends in this place, which was still strange to her. Without friends, Cathy was sure life wouldn't be worth living.

Till nine o'clock, the staff in the Medical Center had the place to themselves. Cathy was only one of half a dozen receptionists who worked in shifts. After patching up her wounds, she prepared the desks in the doctors' rooms, dusting and tidying and changing their date stamps. After that, there were the medical cards of prospective patients to check up and telephone messages to take.

After the doctors on duty arrived, the pace became fast and furious. At first, Cathy had felt she would never get used to it. Instead of an enclosed office, she worked with others in a large, open space with everyone's eyes on her, including those of the waiting patients with nothing to do but watch and listen. It made her self-conscious, until she realized that they were thinking more of their own troubles than of her.

Besides, there was the need to concentrate, so many things happened at once. A doctor's light would go on, the telephone ring, and a new arrival appear at the desk all at the same time. Doctors had priority, of course. She didn't need to be told that, being a doctor's daughter herself.

This morning she was on duty with Hilda Baxter, an older girl who had proved to be a good friend and instructor.

"I've a feeling this is going to be a hectic day," Hilda prophesied. "We'll have to keep our cool!"

Her forecast was right. One of the doctors was called out on an emergency and timetables went awry. Cathy was on the phone taking an appointment, when the light for the next patient appeared. Laying down the phone, she called the patient's name, then finished the call. By this time, a line of new arrivals had formed. Ticking off their names in the appointment book, she asked them to be seated.

"Name, please?" A girl had thrust herself to

the head of the line, her expression petulant, her eyes darting fire.

"I've already given you my name. It's Carr, Celia Carr. My appointment was due half an hour ago. Why am I kept waiting?"

"I'm sorry," said Cathy patiently. "There's been a hold-up. It won't be long now." But the soft answer did not work.

"It's been too long already! My turn must be next."

Consulting the appointment list, Cathy replied firmly—"There are several people before you, I'm afraid."

Her face darkened. Such a lovely face, to scowl like that!

"I'm sure you can do something about it. I'm not used to being kept waiting!"

"Sorry. There are others waiting besides you, you know."

The girl leaned forward. "You refuse to oblige me? No doubt you have your favorites."

"Nothing of the kind. Will you please take a seat?"

Celia Carr turned away, with the retort— "I'll not forget this!" Then, instead of waiting, she marched to the door and stamped out. A lot of good that would do her if she were really ill!

But Cathy suspected there was nothing much the matter. Not that there was any time to reflect on the incident. Darting from desk to filing cabinet, then back to the telephone, she answered questions from patients and doctors, calmed fractious children, and reassured anxious parents. It went on non-stop until at long last the place emptied, the doctors dashed out to their cars, and all was peace.

"Thank goodness that's over," breathed Hilda, subsiding on to a chair. "I'm completely exhausted. How about you?"

Cathy was pulling on her jacket. "Me, too. Still, I like the job, except when people are difficult." She was thinking of Celia Carr.

The other nodded. "We certainly see plenty of life!"

They parted and Cathy took her way across the Square where Aunt Jessie was closing the shop for the dinner hour. At table, after satisfying the first pangs of hunger, Cathy suddenly giggled.

"Such an adventure, Auntie! I came a cropper on the Drummonds' steps, on top of the milk bottles, and who do you think picked me up?"

"Susan Brodie, I expect," responded her aunt.

"Wrong. It was none other than the son of the house."

"Mr. Neil? So he's home!"

"Yes, and he's terribly nice. Not a bit fishy."

Aunt Jessie laughed. "He never was. Shy as a lad, but I expect he's come out of his shell. He was better off getting away from here after that girl let him down. He was very much in love with her, they said."

"I didn't know. Who was the girl?" asked Cathy.

"Celia Carr. She's still around. She jilted the next one, too."

CHAPTER TWO

CATHY WOKE with a start, switched on the bed-light, and peered at the clock beside her. Why had the alarm not rung? Then she remembered that she had not set it last night because there was no need. This was a free morning. Her shift at the Medical Center started at two and went on till the end of evening hours.

Well, she would treat herself to a few more minutes in bed. It was pleasant just to lie still for a while and let one's thoughts drift. In imagination she could hear, above the sounds in Nethershaw's main street, the swish of waves washing up on the shore, the cries of hungry seabirds. These were the sounds that used to wake her back home in Kilgower. Would she ever wake to them again?

She had left her father's house very much against his will. But their loving relationship, broken up by his new wife, seemed gone for ever. His last words had been angry ones; it would be impossible to go back to that atmosphere ever again.

But Cathy was not one to brood. She had begun a new life and was going to make the most of it. She had a good home with Aunt Jessie, an interesting job, and was fast making new friends.

24

The latest of these was Neil Drummond of Airlie House across the Square. Her mind went back to the day of their meeting on the icy doorstep—undignified, to say the least! She had not seen him since, for Susan Brodie had taken in the paper each following morning. Disappointing really, for he looked like a person worth knowing. Never mind, she was bound to bump into him sometime, if fate decreed. Cathy was a great believer in "fate."

Now, indeed, it was time to get up. Slipping her feet into her slippers, she pulled on her robe and went through to the kitchen. There, she put on the kettle and the cereal pan for Aunt Jessie was still downstairs in the shop serving her first customers.

When the water boiled, Cathy stirred in the oatmeal, which had been steeping overnight, and all the time she sang to herself the Hebridean songs she loved so well. Her singing had always irritated her stepmother, but Aunt Jessie didn't mind.

"Westering home with a song in the air." The rhythm went well with stirring the oatmeal. It was sure to taste better, being sung to.

When Aunt Jessie came up from the shop, the cereal was ready to pour.

"Thanks, Cathy! I haven't had a minute to see to breakfast." Her hands were frozen, the tip of her nose pink as usual on a cold morning. "Get you dressed now, honey, and I'll do the rest."

In a short time they were having breakfast at the window which overlooked the street.

Down there they could see by the tall lamps, the early risers going to work. It was a window upon life, said Aunt Jessie, as good as the movies. Indeed, it was this window as much as anything that had made her determined to stay where she was and refuse Andrew Drummond's offer to buy her property.

Breakfast over, Cathy urged—"Let me look after the shop this morning! I guess you'd like to go on a shopping spree. You don't get much chance."

"Just as well; my money stays in my pocket," observed her aunt. "But I'll accept your offer and I promise to waste no time in gossiping. I'll dart in somewhere if I see anybody I know."

Leaving instructions, she proceeded to don her much worn fur jacket and suede boots and set off with her shopping bag while Cathy got down to business. By this time, she knew where most of the stock was kept. Besides papers and magazines, Jessie sold sweets and lemonade, even greeting cards. Also, in hidden corners, there were articles of a vintage you could not get elsewhere for love nor money.

As usual, the forenoon customers were mostly housewives expecting to have a chat with Jessie but quite glad to make the acquaintance of her niece. It was during a lull that Cathy looked up from the accounts ledger to serve a newly arrived customer. She recognized her immediately as Celia Carr, the girl who had been so rude to her at the hospital a few days ago.

Under the scarlet hood of her jacket, Celia's dark hair curled attractively round her face.

Her eyes, gray-green and long lashed, had a seductive beauty and her mouth an alluring curve. Cathy had not expected to see her so soon again.

The newcomer hardly cast a glance at her. She was scanning the shelves.

"Don't tell me you haven't got cigarettes," she complained.

"Sorry. That's about the only thing we don't sell."

"Why not?" Colia demanded.

"There's a tobacconist next door," explained Cathy.

"Oh." Their eyes met. "Why, I've seen you before somewhere."

"That's right. At the Medical Center."

"Of course. You kept me waiting."

"Not my fault—" Cathy began.

"You let other people go in before me. If I had been really ill, you'd have had something to answer for!"

Ruffled by her attitude, "Weren't you really ill?" Cathy replied.

"I was ill enough!"

"Well, I'm glad to see you're better now," was the calm response.

A slight pink tinged the other's cheeks. "And you? Have you lost your job, or what?"

"Not at all. I'm merely helping out in my aunt's shop."

"I see." A long stare. "So you are Jessie Paterson's niece. Well, well."

As she spoke, the door opened to admit another customer. Standing with her back to the door,

Celia did not see him but Cathy did. She found herself face to face with Neil Drummond.

Neil showed no signs of the confusion which she herself felt. As if he had known her all his life, he greeted her with a smiling—"Hello!"

Cathy smiled back at him, and then Celia turned round. For a second her breath seemed taken away, and at the same time Neil stiffened, the smile wiped off his face.

Face radiant, Celia took a step toward him. "This is a great surprise! I thought you were in America!"

"I was," he replied briefly. "I've come home. How are you, Celia?"

"Oh, I'm all right. I heard about your father, Neil. Was that why you came home?"

"The main reason." He came forward to the counter, and with a perturbed glance at Cathy, purchased a weekly magazine, explaining—

"It's for my mother, she loves the stories. I hope you're none the worse for your adventure the other day?"

She laughed. "Not at all. I'm tough."

Celia Carr was still there, obviously waiting for him. Cathy had the impression that he did not want her to wait. Surely he must hate her for jilting him as she had done. Or perhaps he was still in love, or would be, if she encouraged him?

Neil took his change, seemed about to speak further, then with the entrance of another customer, he turned away. Celia joined him and they went out of the shop together.

Neil Drummond walked stiffly beside his companion, searching for an excuse to leave her. He remembered too well the agonies he had gone through in the past, when nothing counted but Celia, the object of his youthful passion. Every word she spoke, the way she used to tantalize him; how they used to quarrel and make up—he remembered it all.

Her face upturned to his, she said softly—

"It's lovely to meet you again, Neil! I've never forgotten you, you know," and she laid her hand on his arm. "I've got a lot of explaining to do, I'm afraid."

"I don't want an explanation, Celia. Everything is past and buried."

"Not for me," she sighed. "Whatever you say, I do want to explain! But not here. There's a new coffee house round the corner. It's quiet there. Come on!"

People were looking at them with interest, so he allowed himself to be led to the coffee house. Finding a corner behind a screen, Celia ordered coffee for both and held out her left hand toward him.

"You see! No ring."

"I had heard," he said coolly.

With lowered eyes—"Neil, I'd just like you to know. I made the biggest mistake of my life when I gave you up for Norman Blyth."

"We all make mistakes," was all he could find to say.

"I wish you had stayed at home! We could have patched things up long ago. I never loved Norman the way I loved you."

He said, quite gently—"We can't relive the past, Celia. Best to forget."

The girl came with the coffee and Celia began to pour it.

"You like it black, I remember. And you take two spoonfuls of sugar."

"That's right." He met her eyes as she handed him the cup. Lovely, pleading eyes.

"If I had only known then what I know now!"

He replied awkwardly: "I suppose we all say that at some time in our lives. What are you doing now, Celia? Did you finish your degree?"

They had been students together, commuting to the university in Glasgow.

She shook her head. "I threw up my studies to get married, then I didn't. I've got a part-time job in a nursery school. But about you, Neil. Tell me, have you—" she hesitated—"have you found anyone else?"

"No, Celia, I have not. There's been no time for anything outside my work. Nor will there be. From now on, I'm going to be extremely busy."

Her expressive eyebrows went up. "Dear me. And what is this very important work, may I ask?"

"Lecturing," he replied briefly.

"How dull! You were always going to strike out, do research work."

"I'll be doing that, too, at Loch Creenan," he informed her.

"That sounds more thrilling. More coffee?"

"No, thank you. Do you mind if I go now, Celia? I must get back."

"Well, if you're in a hurry," she said reluctantly. "I'll come too."

He paid the bill and she preceded him into the street. He did not offer to accompany her farther, however.

"I come here quite often for coffee," she hinted. "Perhaps another time?"

"Afraid not, Celia."

She laughed. "Well, you needn't scowl at me! Goodbye, then, Neil. Give your parents my love. I hope your father gets better soon."

He left her with a feeling of relief. The less he saw of Celia the better. In fact, he'd be wise to avoid women altogether. They just complicated one's life, and what he wanted more than anything was to be able to follow his career without such hindrances.

Evening doctors' hours was over. Patients and doctors had departed, and the Center looked bleak and deserted. Cathy and Hilda Baxter were the last to leave. They had been there since two o'clock and it was now seven. Fortunately, they had been able to snatch a cup of tea and a sandwich to stave off their hunger.

Still a few jobs remained: forms to fill in, tomorrow's medical cards to select, and the usual tidying up to do. While they worked, the two girls kept up a conversation.

Though they had been drawn to each other from the first, they were quite unlike in appearance and character. Whereas Cathy was small and slender, Hilda's figure was tall and regal. Her face had a rather gloomy cast while Cathy's always wore that sunny smile. In fact, Hilda took life very seriously and her nature did not have the outgoing quality that made Cathy so well-liked.

Tonight, however, her tongue was loosened.

"Anybody meeting you tonight, Cathy?"

"No, Hilda, I haven't far to go."

"I thought you might have acquired a boy-friend since you came here."

"Give me time!" she laughed. "I'm in no hurry, you know. I'm waiting for a Grand Passion."

The other looked dubious. "It doesn't happen, Cathy."

"It might; you never know. What about you. I see you're wearing a ring."

Her friend twisted the modest little ring round her finger.

"Yes, I've been engaged for four years."

Amazed, Cathy turned from the filing cabinet to stare at her. "And you didn't tell me! But four years; it's a lifetime. Is he abroad or what?"

"Not at all. He's right here in Nethershaw. His name is Charles Ford. He's in the travel agent's office. You may have seen him."

Cathy shook her head. "Never been in there. Why don't you get married, Hilda?"

The other gave a rueful laugh. "Because it's not one of your grand passions, I suppose. I'm fond of Charles, though, but he wants to wait till we can buy a house and all that. Also, his mother is the possessive sort."

"Oh dear, what a pity. I couldn't bear to be engaged all that time. Of course, I'm a rusher and you've got the patience of a saint. I'll bet he doesn't appreciate you."

"Cathy," said the other earnestly, "I'd like you to meet Charles. He's calling for me tonight. He'll be here—" she glanced at the clock—"in five minutes."

"Better hurry, then. Have you put the phone through to Dr. Nairn?"

"I'll do that now." Their last task was to connect up the doctor who would be on call during the night. This done, they were putting on their outdoor things, when Charles came in from the street.

He was a square-set young man with smooth hair and a rather prim expression. In fact, he looked like a person with no fun in him at all. Wouldn't do for me, thought Cathy, but then I'm not Hilda.

"Ready?" he asked unsmilingly in Hilda's direction.

"Just about. This is Cathy Paton, Charles."

"I see. Pleased to meet you." He took Cathy's hand, let it drop, and went on—"Hilda has told me about you. How do you like living in Nether-shaw?"

"Very much. It's a cozy little town."

"Cozy, in weather like this!" He was wearing a big woolly scarf, and Cathy had a picture of his mother knitting it for him.

"I didn't mean that kind of cozy. It's small and compact and people know each other," she explained.

"Too well, they do. I never knew such a place for gossip. Come on, Hilda, get that coat on."

Bossy, too, reflected Cathy. He didn't even help her while she struggled with her coat sleeves; she herself did that. Then they locked up and went out to the chilly night air and the lights of Drummond Square, crossing over to Jessie Paterson's shop, which of course was shut. When this was the case, the entrance to the flat was through a narrow gangway, and it was here they halted, near a bus stop.

Hilda said goodnight. "Charles and I will be taking the bus."

"Not at all. We'll walk," declared her fiancé. "Do us good."

"But, Charles, I'm tired."

"Tired, with a cushy job like yours! Take deep breaths and you'll be all right."

With a pale smile at Cathy, Hilda took his arm and they walked smartly into the night.

Cathy went thoughtfully upstairs. Was it possible that Charles grudged the bus fares? Poor Hilda. Better never to marry at all than to be tied to a man like that. The man I marry, she mused, would have to be generous and sympathetic, with a sense of humor; all the things that Charles Ford was not. When she met this person, the prince of her dreams, she would know him at once.

In fact—the realization came in a blinding flash—she had actually met him already! As she turned the key in the lock of Aunt Jessie's flat, her heart was thudding alarmingly, and it wasn't just from climbing the stairs.

Cathy had every alternate Saturday free. It was a chance to do some cleaning and washing and sometimes to explore the hills above Nethershaw. And, of course, she could give her aunt a hand in the shop. That was where she was this Saturday when Susan Brodie, the Drummond's housekeeper, staggered in with a heavy load of shopping.

"I can't go another step!" Panting, she sank onto the chair at the counter. "Let me rest a minute, Jessie."

"Rest as long as you like; we don't charge for it," said Jessie good-naturedly. "Have you any more errands to do? I'm sure Cathy would help."

"I'm finished," puffed Susan. "It's the thought of that last slope up to the house that beats me. I'll be all right in a minute."

Gradually, her breath steadied and her cheeks became less flushed.

"You go at it too hard," Jessie declared. "It's a big house, that. You shouldn't have to shop as well as cook and clean."

"Ach, I like shopping. It gets you out. Mrs. Drummond offered to do it, but she worries about the Mister when she's not there. He misses her; I never knew a man so dependent. Of course, he's had a bad shake." She added mournfully—"It's my guess he'll never get over it."

"I'm real sorry," commented Jessie. "If I had known, I might not have said the things I did. We had a bit of a row, you know, the day before he took ill. I've heard the old lady is blaming me."

"It would have happened anyway," Susan affirmed. "You were quite right to give him *laldy;* he hadn't treated you fair. You stick by your wee shop; we couldn't do without it." Susan began to collect her parcels. "Well, I'd better be on my way."

Cathy had been standing by. "Give me that heavy bag, Miss Brodie. I'll carry it for you."

"Will you, honey?" A smile wreathing her plump face, she continued, "I must say your aunt's very lucky to have you."

"Oh, ay, Cathy's a great help," put in Jessie. "Don't hurry back, lassie. Take a *dauner* to yourself."

As they went round the corner and across the Square to the imposing old house, Susan said—

"We'll go in by the back," and she led the way through the yard, quiet on this Saturday afternoon, to the steps at the back of the house. Through a passage, they came to a large kitchen. Though partly modernized, it had a pleasant Old-World atmosphere, with shelves all round, a well-scrubbed table, and a set of shiny dish-covers on the wall. There was linoleum on the floor and a colorful rag rug at the fireplace.

"Sit you down, lass, and I'll make a cup of tea."

Before doing so, Susan carefully inserted a poker into the smothered fire until a thin flame shot up, soon changing the black dross into a red glow. Cathy sat on a wooden chair with a high back, and as she waited, a sense of contentment stole through her. "I love a kitchen that can be lived in," she observed. "We've got one at home in Kilgower, dish-covers and all. I used to enjoy polishing them. I kept house for my father, you know."

"And did you like that better than going out to work?" asked Susan as she handed her a mug of tea.

"Much better. I never really wanted to be anything but a homemaker."

"Not a bad thing to be. Have a pancake! Mrs. Drummond made them. She's good at pancakes."

"Lovely," said Cathy, taking a bite. At that moment the kitchen door opened and a dark head appeared round it.

"It's yourself, Mr. Neil; come on in!" invited Susan.

"But you've got company," said Neil, hesitating.

"It's just Cathy Paton. You know her, don't you?"

"Yes, of course I do, though I didn't know her name till this minute. Good afternoon, Cathy!" He stepped inside.

"Good afternoon." Her voice was husky. She hadn't expected him to be at home and certainly not to appear in the kitchen.

"There's a cup left in the pot," offered Susan.

"I thought there might be." His dark eyes twinkled at Cathy. "I remember Susan's old addiction, you see."

"It's better than some addictions anyway," the housekeeper retorted. "And you're *gey* fond of a *cuppa* yourself."

Perching himself on a high stool, he accepted the mug she offered while Cathy, with a sudden rush of shyness, faltered—"I'll have to go soon. Aunt Jessie will need me."

"Just because I'm here?" he teased. "Surely not. Stay and talk. Please!"

"I'll listen," decided Cathy, "if you do the talking."

"Oh dear, I'm no good at talking. I just lecture."

"Well," put in Susan, "you can lecture us."

"About fish," ventured Cathy.

He laughed, then went on seriously—"My head's full of fish at the moment, to tell the truth. Now, don't laugh, Susan. We're going to be very dependent on fish in the future. There's a population problem you know. We're using up the world's resources far too quickly."

Her interest aroused, Cathy inquired—"But won't all the fish be used up, too?"

He nodded. "Yes, unless we encourage fish farming in Scotland as elsewhere."

Launched on his subject, he went on to tell them about the proposed research to be done at Loch Creenan to find if it would be suitable for fish farming.

"It depends upon what nutrients we find there. That's my job."

Cathy listened intently until he came to a sudden stop.

Cathy was struck dumb. Celia Carr, the girl who had shown such impatience and real nastiness at the hospital that morning. How could a really super man like Neil Drummond be in love with a girl like that? Or did he not know what she was really like? Perhaps love had blinded him.

"What a bore I am! Forgive me. It's your turn now, Cathy."

"Ay, tell us about your home in Kilgower," urged Susan.

"Yes, do," he rejoined; so with his eyes on her, Cathy began the praises of her Highland village.

"Such a lot goes on there, you wouldn't believe! Dances and songfests and so on. I used to sing at them. I was happy there."

"Why did you leave, then?" inquired Neil.

Her smile dimmed. "Oh, Dad married again, and it was all spoiled. But no matter—" the smile flashed out again—"I'm happy here, too."

"Some folk make their own happiness," commented Susan. "Won't you sing something for us now?"

She hung back until Neil added his plea. "Yes, come on, I'd love to hear you."

"What will I sing, then?"

Susan suggested her favorite, "Loch Lomond," and they all joined in at the end.

Me and my true love will never meet again, on the bonnie, bonnie banks of Loch Lomond.

As the last words died away, Susan sighed— "It's so sad! Give us something cheery now."

So Cathy entertained them with "Mairi's Wedding" and other lilting songs. The time passed unnoticed until they became aware that another listener had come on the scene. She was standing just inside the door, a formidable figure leaning on her silver headed cane: Neil's grandmother.

Cathy stopped singing, Neil got to his feet, and Susan began to clear away the tea things.

"You seem to be enjoying yourselves," observed Esther Drummond dryly. "No need to stop for me."

Neil said lightly—"Just a little light relief, Gran! Cathy was singing for us."

"Indeed. And who may Cathy be?" she asked, subjecting her to a detailed scrutiny.

"Jessie Paterson's niece. Cathy, meet my grandmother."

Cathy smiled and extended her hand, but the old lady's remained firmly on her stick.

"Jessie Paterson, eh? So you're another of that ilk. I'm surprised to see you in this house."

Neil spoke up: "Oh come, Gran. Dad and Jessie don't see eye to eye, I know, but why should that affect Cathy?"

"What's bred in the bone," declared the other. "Susan! I hope you're not forgetting it's nearly teatime."

"I'm not in the habit of forgetting," was the starchy reply.

"That's all right, then. Neil, I'd like to speak to you."

"Later, Gran!"

Mrs. Drummond hesitated for one more penetrating glance at Cathy before turning away.

Cathy was on her feet, making for the back door. "I'll really have to go." Her cheeks were burning.

Neil followed her, protesting—"Not that way! I'll show you out by the front."

"No, thanks. I came in by the back and I'll

go out that way. I'm kitchen company after all."

"You're annoyed with us," he said ruefully. "Please don't mind my Gran! She's a prickly old lady, but her bark's worse than her bite. I've enjoyed the 'kitchen company,' Cathy. You have a very sweet voice."

"Thank you. I love to sing. Goodbye then, Mr. Drummond."

"Neil, please. I'll be seeing you again, I hope."

"Yes, I hope so, too." She left him and began her walk across the Square in a daze. He liked her singing. He hoped to see her again. Wonderful!

Then common sense intervened. He was only being polite. Though living so near to each other, there were many things to keep them apart. His grandmother had made that clear.

And there was Celia Carr. She was the kind of girl who really attracted him. That she was still in love with him had been very obvious that day they met in the shop. No doubt they would soon make up their differences.

"I'll have to try very hard not to fall in love with him. It will just bring heartache," she thought, knowing full well that the harm had been done already.

CHAPTER THREE

LATER IN THE DAY of Cathy's visit to the kitchen of Airlie House, the four Drummonds were still seated at table after their evening meal.

Old Mrs. Drummond, stiffly erect as usual, cast her eye round the table.

"Well, if you're all finished, I'll ring for Susan to clear away."

"No need, Gran," interposed her daughter-in-law. "I'll do it myself. Susan has had a busy day."

"Not too busy to drink tea in the afternoon and entertain a visitor," declared the other, rising to ring the bell, which stood on a table at the door. There was a bell set in the wall, but the wire connecting it with the kitchen was broken, like so many relics in the old house.

"A visitor? Don't tell me Susan has a secret admirer."

"She's a bit long in the tooth for that," said her mother-in-law dryly. "No, this was a girl— Jessie Paterson's niece. Neil seems pretty friendly with her, too," and she cast a censorious glance at her grandson.

He returned the look. "I just happened to go

into the kitchen while she was there, Gran. She helped Susan with her shopping, I believe."

"A good excuse to worm her way into this house!"

Neil frowned. "What an unkind remark! I'm surprised at you, Gran. Why should a kind action have an ulterior motive?"

His father had picked up the drift of the conversation.

"I want nothing to do with any relation of Jessie Paterson! Susan ought not to have encouraged her!"

Attempting to rise from the table, he suddenly stumbled. Neil darted to his side.

"Here, take my arm," and he led him to his chair by the fire. "Are you all right, Dad?"

"Ay, as right as I'll ever be. But don't mention that woman's name to me again!"

Neil was about to point out that it was not he but his grandmother who had brought up Jessie's name; but to start an argument was useless. In any case, Susan had arrived with the tray. When she had gone out and things were settled again, the old lady asked to be helped upstairs. Mostly she scorned help and when she asked for it, it was because she had something else on her mind. Thus it was tonight.

"My reading lamp's out of action," she told Neil when they reached her room with its high windows and old-fashioned furniture. "Will you mend it for me? There's a screwdriver in that drawer."

From her high-backed chair she watched him unscrew the plug of the lamp and reconnect

the wires. "We haven't had a real talk since
you came home, Neil, and there will be less
time than ever when you start your college
work on Monday."

"That's right. Was there anything in particular
you wished to talk about?"

"Yes, there's your future."

"My future is nicely in hand, thank you."
His tone was light. He would have to be patient
with Gran, as with his parents. Adapting himself
again to home life was not proving easy, but
he had not expected it to be otherwise.

"Nobody's future is 'in hand,' " was the nippy
reply. "We never know what tomorrow might
bring."

"True." He grinned at her. "So why worry?"

"One has to plan, in case. There's myself, for
instance. I might be gone tomorrow."

"So might we all."

"You know what I mean! I'm eighty. Did you
ever picture yourself at the age? You feel more
out of life than in it."

He patted her hand. "Nonsense, Gran. You're
as full of life as anybody I know."

She gave his hand a little slap. "You've got
to take me seriously! There will be long years
ahead for you when I'll not be here, so avail
yourself of my wisdom now. I've acquired quite
a lot, you know."

"I'm sure of it," he said, going over to press
the lamp plug into its socket. A soft glow
spread from the red-shaded lamp.

"Good! You can put off the main light now.
This is enough to talk by, and electricity's

dear." She took up her knitting and went on—"I never dreamt I would have to economize in my old age, but my nest egg is dwindling and I refuse to live off your father. What with one thing and another, he's in a bad way. Sit down, Neil."

Accepting the inevitable, he obeyed. "When Dad's a bit better, I intend to go into business matters with him. Perhaps it isn't as bad as you think."

She sniffed. "Every bit as bad! I had a word with his accountant." She would, of course. "This place is going to rack and ruin, Neil. It's your heritage and it ought to be preserved. If I thought Airlie House could be restored to its former glory, I would die happy. It lies entirely with you."

"Me? But I haven't got the money to restore it."

"I didn't think you had. There's only one thing for it. You'll have to marry money."

He laughed. "What an old-fashioned notion! People marry for love nowadays."

"And are they any happier? Love is blind. You were in love once yourself and ought to know. Admit it, you wouldn't have been happy married to Celia Carr."

All too true, but he wouldn't give her the satisfaction of admitting it, merely remarking—"One never can tell."

"Of course one can tell! Now, Neil—" she pointed a knitting needle at him—"you're a very good-looking young man, quite a catch. You could have almost any girl, rich or poor."

He shook his head, amused. "Spare my blushes! Girls haven't got time for me. I am no gallant, just a serious-minded scientist."

"Rubbish. Celia Carr was daft about you once, and she would be again if I know anything. I noticed, too, how that Cathy girl was looking at you this afternoon. And you were quite taken with her, too. I can read the signs."

"You read signs that aren't there, Gran. Is that all you've got to say?"

"Not quite. Just you wait till you find a girl with a good *tocher*, Neil. I hope you know what a '*tocher*' is?"

"A dowry, of course. How mercenary would you have me?"

"Not mercenary, sensible. Steer clear of pretty little fly-away girls like Jessie Paterson's niece. She'll do you no good. Besides, there's your father to consider. The very mention of Jessie gets him all upset."

"It was you who mentioned her, not me."

Unabashed—"Whoever it was, he took it badly, so be careful!"

Feeling he had had enough, Neil rose. "I'll be careful! Really, Gran, you're making a mountain out of a molehill."

With all her wisdom, he might have added, she had never learned not to interfere. But she was old and rather frail-looking tonight, so he did not say it. Picking up her ball of wool, he laid it beside her.

"I've got things to do. Shall I switch on your radio?"

"Yes, please." But when a gust of rock music

throbbed out, she protested—"Put it off! Quick!"

"I'll try another program—"

"No, there's never anything good. Nothing good, anywhere."

Sorry for her, he bent to kiss her. "Cheer up! You'll feel better tomorrow."

With a little smile, she patted his hand. "You're a good lad, Neil. I'm glad you came home."

After doing some preparation for Monday, Neil went down to join his parents. His father was half asleep, a frail hand resting on each arm of his chair, his head sunk low on his chest. His mother was reading the magazine he had bought in Jessie Paterson's shop. He noticed anew the white streaks in her hair, the worried lines on her face.

One thing Evelyn Drummond lacked was confidence in herself. Compliant by nature, she had given in all along to her strong-minded husband and mother-in-law. Now, Neil realized, it was too late for her to take a stand of her own; nor would she ever want to.

"Enjoying the stories, Mom?"

She looked up with a smile. "Yes, Neil. They all end happily. That's what I like."

"Some people would say life's not like that."

"Perhaps not, but there's always hope. A happy ending in a story gives you hope."

"Quite right. Wishes do sometimes come true."

She nodded. "Indeed they do. I wished that you would come home and here you are."

He sat down beside her and took her hand.

"Perhaps I ought not to have left at all. It's not as if I had a brother or sister to keep you company."

"I used to long for a daughter," she said, "but it wasn't to be. Perhaps someday, Neil, you'll bring a girl home to brighten up the place."

His eyes twinkled. "In the remote future, perhaps. What you need now is to get out and about more. Dad's car is in for a checkup, but I'll be able to take you for a run next Saturday. We might go to Loch Creenan."

"Good! And Neil, tomorrow's Sunday. Will you come to church with me?"

"Of course I'll come with you!"

"Thanks." Her eyes were very bright. He got a glimpse of how she used to look when he was a boy. "It will be lovely to have you in the pew. I'm so proud of my clever son!"

His father stirred and opened his eyes. "Evelyn?"

She was at his side in a moment. "Yes, Andrew?"

"I'm tired. Help me to bed, please."

Together, they assisted him to the room on the ground floor which had been adapted for his convalescence. There were many little things to do for him, which he would have preferred to do for himself, and the frustration made him so short-tempered it was hard to be patient. Yet, reflected Neil, his mother had tended him day and night for long weeks with never a grumble. Women such as she were taken for granted. Few ever sang their praises, especially in this day of liberation.

On Sunday mornings the streets of Nethershaw had none of the bustle of weekdays. In the Square all was hushed. There wasn't even the tinkle of milk bottles, as Sunday's milk was delivered on Saturdays.

As the pale dawn strengthened and the street lights went out, there might be the swish of a passing car, but there was no real stir until the church bells began to ring.

From his bedroom window, Neil could see the first comers making their way across the Square to the church with the tall, tapering spire where his family had worshipped for generations. There was permanence there, he thought—that church and what it stood for, unchanged and unchanging in a confused and changing world.

His mother was waiting for him in the hall dressed in her muskrat coat, reminder of better days. "This is a red-letter day for me, Neil!"

"I hope there will be many," he said, taking her arm down the steps.

In the church porch they were welcomed by the elders on duty, men whom Neil remembered well. It might have been yesterday that he last shook hands with them; was it really five years? The rich, swelling notes of the organ filled the church as they took their seats in the family pew. It was all so familiar; even the minister had not altered in appearance—nor in the content of his sermon, for that matter.

The choir, too. Gray-haired basses, a sprin-kling of tenors, aging contraltos, and a few newcomers among the sopranos. He recognized one of them— yes, it was Cathy Paton, whose sweet singing had so delighted Susan and himself the day before. He had a chance to study her today when she did not know he was looking. Her profile was toward him; neat nose, smiling lips, pointed chin. He had not noticed before how lovely her hair was; probably she'd had it tied back, but today it was loose on her shoulders, escaping from her green beret in a cascade of gold.

There, he had to check himself. Steady on, Neil! Before you know it you'll be letting that girl monopolize your thoughts, and you can't afford to do that. No way!

He shifted his gaze to turn to a hymn, but the minute they stood up to sing, his eyes were on her again. How earnest she looked, her whole heart in her singing, the sweet high tones of her voice like sparkling drops of foam on the crest of a wave. Oh dear, there he was again. Drops of foam, indeed: it wasn't like him at all to go all poetical. Besides, he couldn't really hear her voice above the rest; it was all imagination.

The service over, he and his mother were caught up at the church gate by a group of well wishers inquiring about his father's health and expressing pleasure at his own homecoming. At last they got free, only to come face to face with two people emerging from another gate—

Cathy and her aunt. His hand on his mother's arm, he stopped to greet them. Jessie Paterson looked uncertain, as if she would like to carry on without delay, but on second thoughts she returned his greeting and so did Cathy, with a shy glance at his mother.

"Mother, you know Cathy's aunt; well, this is Cathy."

Fearing his mother might not respond, he was relieved when she murmured a quiet—"How do you do?" As they were all going the same way, they walked on together, Neil with Cathy, the two women behind.

Jessie felt most uncomfortable. Not that she had anything against Mrs. Drummond, poor soul, but she probably had been told to have nothing to do with that awful Jessie Paterson, or her niece either.

"So you've joined the choir," Neil was saying to Cathy. "Quite an acquisition."

"Oh, I don't know. My voice is very light-weight."

"Compared with some of our unrestrained sopranos, it is, but none the worse for that. And how is the work at the Medical Center going?"

"I enjoy it," she told him, "except when things get hectic, and they can, you know."

"I believe you. But I can't see you getting flustered."

Cathy chuckled. "Come in at a busy time and you will! But I'm sure you'll have no need. You look as if nothing would ever ail you."

Neil murmured something about tempting

providence by making statements like that, but they had now reached the steps of Airlie House. The others joined them, and with a brief farewell Jessie and Cathy walked on to their flat above the shop. Jessie's telltale nose was very pink.

"I'm sorry if you didn't want to meet Mrs. Drummond, Auntie, but it couldn't be helped, could it?"

"I suppose not. Ach, the devil, she's not to blame for the awkwardness. But the less we see of her the better. Ay, and that applies to Mr. Neil as well. Don't you be taking a notion to him, Cathy!"

"Me?" she asked, her cheeks flaming. "What put that into your head?"

"Ever since that day you fell on their steps and spilled the milk, you've turned all fey at the mention of his name."

"You're imagining things," she declared.

"No, I'm just observant. He's a lovely man, Cathy, but it would never do."

"I don't understand."

"Yes you do. You couldn't ever be anything to Neil Drummond, so you might as well realize that right now."

Cathy was silent. Aunt Jessie was just putting ideas into her head. Not for a minute would she have admitted that the ideas were already there.

Celia Carr had been at church that morning, too, sitting beside her mother in their pew at the back. Not a regular church-goer, she had come in the hope that Neil might be there and she'd get a chance to speak to him, for since their parting at the coffee shop, there had been no further encounter.

All she got in church was the back view of his head, but that was enough to bring back all the old longing. What had been a romantic attachment in the old days, easily cast off, had on his return from abroad, grown stronger. Celia's deeper feelings were now involved. More than anything in the world, she longed to get things back on the old footing.

Her hopes of speaking to Neil after the service were dashed, however. There were too many people around him, and his mother was in full possession. Celia had once been very friendly with both his parents, a welcome visitor to Airlie House. Since the breakup, she had not been near, unsure of her reception.

Mrs. Carr, guessing at what was in her daughter's mind, remarked dryly—"Your old friend is back, I see."

"Yes," was the reply. "I had coffee with him one day."

"You didn't tell me." Celia never told her anything; she was a law to herself. Though Mrs. Carr and her daughter never openly quarrelled, they were always on prickly terms with each other.

"I didn't think you'd be interested," was the cool reply.

"Of course, I'm interested. Worried, too. You don't seem to know what to do with your life, Celia."

"Oh, don't start to preach, please! We get enough of that in church."

It was when they were crossing the street that Celia looked back. Neil and his mother had left the crowd and were walking on in the company of Jessie Paterson and her niece.

Mrs. Carr also had turned. "That's a strange thing! I thought there was a kind of feud there, yet they seem quite friendly. Especially Neil and the niece. I've seen her at the Medical Center. A charming girl."

"If that's your opinion, it isn't mine," snapped her daughter.

Mrs. Carr said no more. It was all too obvious that Celia was jealous. Since her teenage days, her daughter had been difficult and now, it seemed, there was more trouble ahead. Why couldn't she have the kind of daughter who would confide in her, ask her advice? Celia never did that. In many ways, they were strangers.

Could she have seen into her daughter's mind at that moment, she might have been more disturbed. The sight of Neil with Cathy Paton had been a distinct shock to Celia. If she did not do something quickly, she would lose him forever, if not to Cathy, then to some other girl. On the way home her mind was busy. She would have to make friends with the family again. She could make the excuse of inquiring after his father's health. Yes, she would do it tomorrow.

Next day, on leaving her part-time job at the nursery school, Celia went straight to the florist's in the main street and bought a large bunch of early daffodils. With these in her hand, she rang the bell of Airlie House.

Susan Brodie opened the door. The visitor stepped forward—

"Good afternoon! I called to inquire after Mr. Drummond. How is he?"

"He's coming on all right," was the curt reply. Susan had never cared much for Neil's fiancée: not nearly good enough for him, and to throw him over like that! Now, here she was again, sweet as sugar, as if nothing had happened.

"I'm so glad. I brought these flowers for him," and she handed them over. "I'd like a word with the invalid, if possible. Could you ask?"

"I suppose so," mumbled Susan. "You'd better come in." Leaving Celia in the hall, she went through to the sitting room. Mr. Drummond was alone, his wife being at a meeting of the church guild and his mother resting upstairs. He was feeling lonely and depressed. At the sight of the daffodils in Susan's hand, his face brightened.

"So spring is on the way. Who brought these flowers, Susan?"

She told him—"Miss Carr. The girl that Mr. Neil—"

"Yes, I remember. Thoughtful of her. Is she still there?"

"Ay, she's asking to see you."

Not many visitors called at the house. There were plenty at the start of his illness but they had dropped off, weary of well-doing. Celia Carr had not done right by Neil, but if she wanted to make amends, he could not turn her away.

"Ask her to come in," he said.

Susan hesitated. "Are you sure you're fit?"

"I'm quite fit," he declared testily. "Need a bit of company, that's all."

Susan returned to Celia. "You can go in, but mind, don't stay long!"

Genuinely touched by the sight of Neil's father in his helpless state, Celia hurried forward to clasp his hand.

"Mr. Drummond, I'm so sorry! I've been thinking about you, believe me, but I didn't like to call before. I don't know what you must think of me."

"I think," he replied in his slow tones, "that it was very kind of you to bring those daffodils. I hadn't realized it was spring. Can you stay and talk to me?"

She took a chair near him, exerting herself to please him. When she liked, Celia could be very charming, and the weary invalid listened with pleasure to her amusing chit-chat, even greeting it with laughter. It was the sound of that laughter that amazed his wife when she opened the door on her return.

"Sorry to have been so long, Andrew!" Then, taken aback—"Oh, it's you, Celia."

"Yes, it's me." She was on her feet, smiling apologetically. "I couldn't stay away any longer. I simply had to see for myself how Mr. Drummond was getting on. But I'll have to go now. I'll come back again, though, if he would like me to."

"Yes," Andrew urged, "do come back and entertain me. The days are so long!"

Celia went on her way, well pleased. The visit had been a success. Seldom in her life had she failed to get exactly what she wanted, and she was confident that things were going to work out her way again.

On the following Saturday, Cathy had her job to go to in the forenoon, but as the Medical Center closed at one, she was free for the rest of the day.

As she crossed the Square to her aunt's flat, she realized that after long weeks of cold and storm, the sun was actually shining, dappling the pavements with light and shadow. It had a curious effect on her. Instead of walking sedately, she began to skip along and only stopped when she noticed that people were looking at her.

Too bad. If she could only go somewhere without people, where she could be as daft and lighthearted as she pleased!

"It's spring fever," declared her aunt when she confessed how she felt. "You'd better get out into the country and work it off."

The advice fitted in with her mood. In slacks and sweater, with stout shoes on her feet, she set off up the hill to explore.

Soon she had traversed the known part of the road and was into a scene which was strange to her. There was a parting of the ways here with a signpost pointing in one direction—"To Glen Fiort" and in the other "To Loch Creenan." There was no doubt in her mind. She would

go and see the loch where Neil was to carry on
his research. Not that he would be there today,
but once she had seen the place, she would be
able to picture him there in future.

On she walked up the road. The trees on
either side were winter bare, which meant one
got glimpses of the scenery. Every season had
its advantages. Now she was at the top of the
incline, looking down on a shining sheet of
water which must be Loch Creenan. That mountain on the far side, still snowbound, would be
Ben Creenan.

At the margin of the loch she stopped, spell-
bound. It was quiet here, not a person in sight.
The white Ben and its neighboring hills were
mirrored in the smooth surface, and there near
the shore two swans floated majestically. The
only movement was a flurry of seagulls swirling
above her head. At the far end of a bay she
could see a jetty with a launch alongside, but
even that was motionless.

The ground on which Cathy stood sloped
steeply down to a pebbly beach. At sight of
those pebbles and the clear, shallow water, she
had a sudden onrush of homesickness. Back
home in her village there were shining pebbles
just like that, the water lapping round them in
a gentle rhythm. She had to get nearer to
listen to that sweet, sad song.

Drawn as by a magnet, Cathy started down
the slope. It was slippery with wet, pulpy
leaves and mossy stones, but as usual she
hastened on regardless. The descent became a
headlong rush—until she found she couldn't

stop herself. There wasn't even a tree trunk she could cling to. With a bump she landed at last, hitting her ankle against a sharp rock.

Lying there among the pebbles, she kept quite still to regain her breath. Then she staggered to her feet, only to drop down again. Pulling up the leg of her slacks, she saw there was blood on her ankle, which had already begun to swell.

"Bother!" she muttered, "oh bother, bother, bother."

Taking off her scarf, she wound it tightly round her ankle and staggered up again. On hands and knees she climbed up to the road and started to walk home. It was agony. She would never get there unless some kind motorist took pity on her.

But the first motorist who passed was in too big a hurry. The second also took no notice of her plight. Number three then appeared; no hope there, either. But wait, the car was slowing down, was stopping just in front of her. She hobbled toward it thankfully.

Inside the car were three people, including the driver, who opened the door and got out to help her. The hand he held out to her was the same hand that had helped her once before on the steps of Airlie House. The hand of Neil Drummond.

CHAPTER FOUR

NEIL DRUMMOND HAD been driving slowly round the margin of Loch Creenan when he caught sight of the girl's figure limping along some distance in front. Beside him in the car, his father was enjoying his first real outing since his illness, and Evelyn Drummond in the back seat was quietly appreciating the beauties of the loch.

"Somebody in distress, I think. Perhaps we should offer her a lift," suggested Neil.

"Faking it, no doubt," was his father's comment. "I'd take no notice if I were you."

But on catching up, Neil realized who the girl was and stopped at once.

"You!" exclaimed Cathy, taking the hand he extended. "Oh, I'm so glad! I've had a fall."

"Hard luck. What's the damage?"

"Plenty! Especially my ankle. Ow!"

She clung to his arm while he opened the rear door of the car and helped her in. Mrs. Drummond moved over.

"You've hurt yourself? Sit down here."

"Thanks," gasped Cathy gratefully. "I'm sorry to give trouble."

"No trouble. We're on our way home. Let me see what's wrong."

Cathy pulled up her trouser leg to reveal a very swollen ankle streaked with blood.

"Oh dear! The sooner that's seen to the better."

Neil glanced behind. "We'll get you patched up at the Medical Center.

Cathy answered ruefully—"It's closed. Saturday afternoon!"

"We'll try the hospital, then. I'll take you home first, Dad."

Mr. Drummond moved uneasily. "Yes, Neil, I'm tired. Who is the girl?"

"Her name is Cathy Paton."

"Oh." His face flushed. "Jessie Paterson's niece, is she?"

"The same. One has got to help, Dad." He kept his voice low.

"Well, as long as one stops there," muttered the other, closing his eyes and sinking into himself.

In spite of Mrs. Drummond's solicitude, Cathy felt ill at ease. Though she could not hear what was said, she sensed that Neil's father resented her presence. Perhaps it was natural. Poor man, he had been very ill and probably Aunt Jessie hadn't minced her words during their quarrel.

Little more was said until Neil drew up at the steps of Airlie House. There, he assisted his parents inside.

"I'll help you into the house, Dad; then I'll take Cathy along to the hospital."

"Do you have to do that?" protested the invalid. "There are plenty of taxis."

Cathy had heard. "Yes, please, I'll take a taxi."

"You'll do no such thing," declared Neil. "Stay there and don't move!"

She had no intention of obeying, however. As they disappeared into the house, she let herself out of the car and stumbled across to the nearby taxi office. She had almost reached it, when Neil's hand gripped her shoulder.

"I told you not to move!"

"I had to," she stammered. "Your father needs you more than I do. I'm quite all right!"

"Don't pretend! Here, take my arm back to the car."

She could only do as he said.

"There—" as he settled her beside him. "Is the hospital still where it was five years ago?"

She nodded assent and they went through the town to the small country hospital on the outskirts, where Neil helped her into the emergency room. She thanked him.

"But please don't wait for me. It's sure to be ages."

"Then I'll wait for ages. Would you like me to phone your aunt?"

"Yes, if you would, but don't alarm her."

"Trust me." With an encouraging grin he left her to locate the telephone in the reception hall. Jessie Paterson, having closed her shop, was back in the flat.

"It's Neil Drummond, Miss Paterson."

"Yes?" Her voice was doubtful. There was something wrong, else why should one of that clan be phoning her?

"Cathy has had a slight accident. Probably just a sprained ankle, but we're having it seen to at the hospital. I thought it better to phone you. I'll bring her back as soon as possible."

"I see. It's kind of you, but I don't understand. Why you, and how did she do it?"

"She'll tell you herself. It was at Loch Creenan. She was in a hurry to get down to the water, I believe."

Jessie snorted. "In a hurry? That's Cathy all over, she just lunges at things."

Chuckling— " 'Lunging' is the word. You're not to worry, Miss Paterson, she'll be all right."

Meanwhile, Cathy was having her injuries seen to by one of the nurses. "There may be a broken bone in that ankle," she was told. "I'd better fetch Dr. Nairn. He just happens to be on the premises."

"Oh, good." The doctor was one of her favorites at the Center. He appeared shortly; a middle-aged man with a gray moustache and quiet eyes.

"Hello, there," he greeted her. "I thought you would know better than to give a busy doctor more work!"

"Yes, I'm sorry," she apologized.

"Let me see the damage." With puckered brow he probed at her ankle. "Well, something may possibly have cracked, but I'd say it was a bad sprain. The X-ray department is closed, but if this doesn't improve come back on Monday. Meanwhile, nurse will bandage you up."

"Thanks," said Cathy, relieved. "If it does

improve, I can go back to work on Monday, can't I?"

"Yes, if you rest tomorrow. Keen on your work at the Center, aren't you? You're picking it up very well."

"Thanks to Hilda Baxter. She is very helpful."

"Yes—" his face lit up. "Miss Baxter is one of the best."

His tone surprised her. She'd had no idea that Dr. Nairn held her friend in such high regard. Or was it more than regard? Of course not. Hilda was Charles Ford's friend; she was just imagining things.

Supplied with a pair of crutches, she joined Neil, waiting patiently on a bench in the entrance hall.

"It's nothing serious," she told him. "Thanks for waiting."

"No bother. I love the informal atmosphere here; so different from those big, impersonal hospitals. Your aunt's expecting you. I don't think she's unduly worried."

On the way home Cathy sat beside him, still shaken from her fall but feeling strangely at ease. She seemed to have known him for a very long time, yet they had only met four times before: first on the steps of Airlie House, then in Aunt Jessie's shop the day Celia Carr appeared. There was also the afternoon she'd gone with Susan Brodie to carry her parcels, and he'd come into the kitchen to have tea and a sing-along. A short meeting on the way home from church was the fourth time. She had counted them all, cherishing them in her heart, they were so precious, those meetings. It was like the song she'd heard Aunt Jessie sing: "The hours I spend with thee, dear heart, are like a string of pearls to me."

"You're very quiet," said Neil in her ear. "Sell your thoughts for a penny?"

She laughed, shaking her head. Not for a thousand pounds would she have confessed!

"I forgot about inflation," he went on. "In any case, I was wrong to ask. Our thoughts are our own property, after all. Still, it's nice to exchange them sometimes, a real test of friendship."

It occurred to him that, full as his life had been, he had never experienced this kind of friendship. Celia had not been interested in the workings of his mind except as regards herself. The generation gap kept him from being fully frank with his parents, and the friendships he had made abroad were only surface deep.

Drawing up at Aunt Jessie's shop, he helped Cathy out of the car. At the foot of the stairs, she had to stop.

"Oh dear, how does one get upstairs with crutches?"

"No need to worry; I'll carry you."

"You can't!"

"Do you think I'm not strong enough?" he demanded.

She looked up at his tall broad-shouldered figure. "Of course you're strong. It's just that, well, it's so undignified."

With a laugh, he picked her up and the crutches went flying.

"I'll come back for those. Put your arms round my neck."

She obeyed, laying her head against his shoulder. Her fine silken hair brushed his cheek as his grasp tightened round her.

"I'm not too heavy?"

"You're like thistledown." When they reached Aunt Jessie's door, he still held her.

"We're here. Put me down, please!"

He felt reluctant to let her go. She seemed to belong there, in his arms, so feminine, so sweet. Not a man to yield to impulse, he did so now. Her lips were near and they were smiling. He bent his head to kiss her, and on impulse, too, she responded with warmth.

At that moment, Aunt Jessie opened the door. She said nothing, just looked aghast. Then Neil set his burden down.

"He had to carry me upstairs," explained Cathy.

"I see. Very kind of him."

"If he hadn't given me a lift, I'd still be staggering home. I'm afraid I've spoiled his afternoon."

"Pity about that. We're much obliged to you, Mr. Drummond. You wouldn't care to come in?" Her tone was distantly polite.

Neil glanced at Cathy but could not read her face.

"No thank you, Miss Paterson. My parents are expecting me."

"Of course you mustn't keep them waiting. Goodbye, then."

Cathy said goodbye too, "And thank you again." He took her hand for an instant, then ran downstairs. There lay the discarded crutches. He picked them up and ran back to catch Cathy as she was closing the door.

"I'm sorry," he whispered urgently. "Are you angry?"

The expression in her bright blue eyes was one he would never forget. There was laughter in it and a tenderness that moved him deeply.

"Not angry," she whispered back, "just happy." Then her aunt took charge and the door was closed.

He went across the Square, lightheaded and full of exultation.

Cathy sank down on the sofa in the living room, her head in a whirl, while Aunt Jessie fetched a footstool to prop up the foot.

"What did they tell you at the hospital?" she inquired.

Cathy told her the verdict. "It might have been worse, you know."

"Why did you have to do such a silly thing at all?"

"I didn't do it on purpose, Aunt Jessie. It was just an accident."

Jessie shook her head. "You're prone to accidents and will be as long as you lunge at things the way you do. Better safe than sorry."

"I know. I'll try to remember," was the meek reply.

"Ay, and there's another thing you'd do well to remember. Either my eyes deceived me when I opened the door, or that man was kissing you."

Cathy's eyes danced. "Quite right, he was. Believe me, I was as surprised as you were."

"Don't tell me that! You must have been leading him on."

"I was not!" protested her niece. "He just did it. What's more, I didn't mind a bit."

Jessie was becoming exasperated. "Well, you ought to have minded. Such light behavior isn't worthy of you, Cathy. I won't have you kissing every Tom, Dick, and Harry that comes along."

"But Neil isn't every Tom, Dick, or Harry! He's himself, and very special."

Her aunt was truly worried. "I was afraid of this. I told you before, the Drummonds' son is not for you. Probably he's just playing with your affections. Men do that, you know."

"Do they really? You sound very Victorian," laughed Cathy.

"Victorian or not, it's the truth. You've got to stop encouraging him. Promise me."

But Cathy was all worked up. What with her fall, the pain she had suffered, and that last incident on the staircase, the last thing she needed was a scolding. Her eyes filled with tears.

"I certainly shan't promise any such thing!"

Seeing her distress, Jessie put an arm round her.

"Don't cry, honey."

Cathy pushed her away. "I'll cry if I like!"

"All right. I'll go and make a cup of tea. You're not yourself," and she went to put on the kettle while Cathy buried her head in the sofa cushion, sorting out her emotions. Perhaps she ought not to have let Neil kiss her, but it had all seemed so natural, a fitting climax to the whole adventure. Anyhow, she couldn't have helped it and neither, she suspected, could he. What was going to happen now? She wouldn't think about it, wouldn't hope too much, but it might be something pretty wonderful.

Next morning, reaction had set in. Cathy felt glued to her bed with exhaustion, and her foot and leg ached miserably. Bringing in her breakfast, Aunt Jessie ordered her to stay put, which she was very pleased to do. Back to sleep again for what seemed hours, she was dimly aware of the telephone ringing and Aunt Jessie answering it. Instinctively, she struggled out of bed to get to the door.

Before she got there, her aunt had replaced the phone.

"Was it Neil?" gasped Cathy.

"Yes, it was, and what are you doing out of bed?"

"I wanted to talk to him. You might have come for me!"

"I thought you were asleep."

"Well, so I was, but even if—. Did he ask to speak to me?"

"When I told him you were resting, he said
not to disturb you. He just wanted to know if
you were all right and I said you were. There
was no need for anything further."

"But there was!" wailed Cathy. "I didn't
thank him properly. I must ring him back."

"You're just as likely to get his mother or
the old dragon herself. How would you like
that?"

She wouldn't like that at all. Perhaps she
shouldn't risk it. Besides, she felt very queer,
as if she might faint any minute.

Aunt Jessie took her arm firmly. "You got
up too suddenly. Back to bed with you!"

She was only too glad to obey.

Next day, to her surprise and relief, Cathy
felt much better. She was even able to put her
foot on the ground without pain. The swelling
had receded, and it was obvious there was no
break, so in the afternoon, armed with her
crutches, she reported for duty.

At first she and Hilda Baxter had the place
to themselves.

"Whatever have you done to yourself?" demanded Hilda.

Subsiding on to a chair, Cathy related yesterday's events, omitting only that all important
kiss.

"Well!" exclaimed the other. "You're lucky,
being rescued so romantically. Neil Drummond
is a real heart throb. To think he actually
carried you up the stairs! It's more than Charles
would do for me. Of course, I'm a heavyweight,
I'd need a superman and Charles isn't that."

"Neil Drummond could do it; he's frightfully strong," boasted Cathy.

The other gave her a knowing look. "So it's happened, the Grand Passion. Oh Cathy, I'm so glad!"

Cathy's cheeks were burning. "Hold on a bit, Hilda, it's not a grand passion yet."

"It's going to be, though, I can sense it."

They were interrupted by the arrival of Doctor Nairn, who stopped on his way through reception to ask Cathy how she was feeling.

"Better? Good. Just take it easy; leave the hard work to Miss Baxter," and he gave Hilda one of his rare smiles.

"That man thinks a lot of you," Cathy told her. " 'One of the best.' That's how he described you at the hospital."

"Really?" said Hilda, surprised. "He's so quiet, you never know what he's thinking. He's a kind of hero, Cathy. Apart from his doctoring, he devotes all his time to a young brother who is handicapped."

"I didn't know. That's why he's so quiet and kind of sad-looking, poor man."

Patients began to arrive and the afternoon's work proceeded. Cathy occupied herself with some book work, which kept her seated, but she found it difficult to drag her mind down to practical matters when it insisted on soaring upward in romantic daydreaming.

Would Neil phone again to inquire after her? Might he suddenly appear at the reception desk, demanding to speak to her? The notion was fantastic, of course, for he was far away, not even thinking of her. Thinking only about his fish, no doubt, and the students he was lecturing to. However, he would get in touch some way, she was sure. When he did, she would not listen to Aunt Jessie's warnings, no indeed!

When Dr. Nairn's office hours were over, he instructed Cathy to go home early.

"You've had enough for one day. Good of you to come at all," he said gratefully.

The days were getting longer now, and it was still daylight when she left the Center. Instinctively, her glance flew across the Square to Airlie House. Perhaps he was coming or going, you never knew! But the person she saw coming down the steps was not Neil. It was Celia Carr.

Cathy stood still, leaning on her crutches. She had almost forgotten about Neil's former fiancée. So Celia was still on visiting terms in that house, a friend of the family, which Cathy certainly was not! Celia was not kitchen company; she came and went by the front door. She was accepted.

All this rushed through her mind as she started to hobble across the street to the shop. She had not reckoned on meeting Celia face-to-face, but the girl went out of her way to inquire—

"Hello, what's this? Had an accident?"

"Sprained my ankle," was the short reply.

"Too bad. Cramp your style a bit, won't it? I'll come along with you to the shop. Might as well buy a paper, now I'm here. I've just been up visiting Neil's father. He likes me to go in for a chat now and then."

"Yes, I'm sure he does."

"You know my fiancé, don't you?" Celia went on.

"Your fiancé?" stammered Cathy. "You mean Neil Drummond? I thought that was off."

With a gay laugh—"Oh well, it was hanging fire a bit while he was away but never really off, as you put it. Now that he's home, it's all right again."

They had reached the shop, which was still open. Aunt Jessie was busy with customers and Cathy went straight through to the back shop to sit down. The weakness she felt had nothing to do with her ankle, however.

Not for a minute did she doubt what Celia Carr had just told her. That the other girl's wishful thinking should lead her to tell a downright lie did not occur to her, though she often indulged in wishful thinking herself.

So that kiss had meant nothing—less than nothing. Aunt Jessie had been right, Neil was just "playing with her affections." His serious attentions were for Celia Carr. "Men are like that." Perhaps they were, but she had set this man on a pedestal, far above the rest.

"I'm stupid and fanciful. What's a kiss after all? It means nothing." But the memory of how she had responded so willingly burned in her. He must think her very cheap.

"Cathy, pet, what's wrong?" Aunt Jessie had come through after closing the shop and was looking at her anxiously. Cathy jerked up her head.

"Nothing's wrong. The work was a bit much for me today, that's all."

Though Jessie had her doubts, she did not show them.

"You should have stayed at home. Too conscientious, that's what you are! Come up now and have tea."

To Jessie, the teapot was a panacea for all ills. But Cathy remained pale and distraught all through the meal, quite different from her usual self.

"There is something wrong, Cathy. Why not be frank with me? I'm here to be a mother to you, you know that."

"Yes, I know, and you have been kind, Aunt Jessie. Go on being kind and don't ask me any more, please."

Her aunt desisted, but after tea she did receive a faint clue. They had settled down to view television, when the phone rang. Cathy stiffened.

"I'll answer it," said Jessie, going into the hall. She was back in a second. "It's Neil Drummond and he wants to speak to you."

Cathy started up, then quickly sank back. "Tell him I can't come."

"Why not? I don't understand."

"You told me not to encourage him. I'm taking you at your word. Go on, Aunt Jessie. Say I'm all right, but I'd rather he didn't call again."

"Well, if you really mean it—"

"Of course I mean it!"

Her aunt went out, and Cathy increased the TV volume so that she would not hear the conversation. Jessie came back still looking puzzled.

"He wouldn't believe me at first. I had to make it quite clear that you didn't want to hear from him again. That was right, wasn't it?"

"Quite right. Thank you, Auntie."

Jessie patted her shoulder. "I'm glad you've come to your senses, honey."

"Yes, I have come to my senses," was the mournful reply.

When Neil Drummond put down the telephone, his first impulse was to rush round to Jessie Paterson's flat and demand to see Cathy. Not that he didn't believe Jessie, but he felt he needed more explanation from Cathy herself.

It seemed to him that perhaps, after all, she had not forgiven him for kissing her. It was a pretty unforgivable thing to do in his code, but she had not objected at the time. In fact, she was happy about it—hadn't she said so?

On thinking it over, her attitude must have changed. She'd seen him as some gay Lothario, kissing girls on the least provocation, when in fact he was strictly abstemious in that respect. He simply could not understand what had made him break his rule. It was a mystery he must probe further by getting to know her better. He'd looked forward to that! He could not imagine anything more delightful than having her as friend and confidante, to counteract the rather depressing atmosphere of Airlie House. Now, it seemed, that was to be denied him.

His spirits at zero, he went to the room that he used as a study and tried to get interested in a textbook about "Aquatic Productivity." It seemed like so much jargon in his present mood and he soon closed it. He would have to do something about Cathy. Yes, he would write to her.

Three times he started a letter. The third version, very short, ran: "My dear Cathy, I can but think you are angry with me and write to apologize. I promise I shan't transgress again if you will be friends. I need a friend like you. Please let me know when I can see you. Sincerely, Neil Drummond."

Addressing the envelope, he went downstairs intending to post it, though unfortunately she would not get it till the day after tomorrow. Usually a patient man, Neil felt impatient. He wanted to get the letter to her now.

Just then, Susan Brodie came through the hall dressed for going out.

"Hello, Susan! Whither bound?"

"Across the Square to see Jessie Paterson," she told him.

A bright idea dawned. "Then you can deliver this note, will you, please? It's for Cathy."

She smiled broadly. "With the greatest of pleasure," and her eyes twinkled meaningfully.

"Now, don't be thinking things," he admonished. "You heard about her accident? It's just an inquiry."

"Sure. Would you want an answer?"

"If she would like to give you one, yes, please."

Susan was thrilled to be the bearer of what she was sure was a love letter. She thought the world of Cathy and had adored Neil since babyhood. This new attachment pleased her far more than his affair with Celia Carr. That girl was selfish to the core, but not wee Cathy, who always considered other people's feelings before her own. She would help his career, not hindor it, as the other would have done.

Jessie was expecting her. It was a weekly visit, never returned because of Jessie's vow never to darken the doors of Airlie House.

"Just hang your coat in the hall, Susan. Cathy's in the room watching TV, though she'd be better in her bed."

"Sorry about her accident," said Susan following her into the room. "Somebody else is sorry, too," and she handed the note to Cathy. "It's from Mr. Neil."

Cathy took it gingerly, while her aunt commented—

"But he phoned earlier! He didn't need to write."

Susan chuckled. "Love's young dream, you know!"

Cathy got up unsteadily. "I'll read this in my room, and it isn't 'love's young dream' at all, Miss Brodie!"

Jessie turned to Susan when she had gone. "What did you say that for? There's no question of anything between these two."

"Ach, that's all you know. I think they're in love."

"Nonsense. I'd never countenance such a thing."

"They wouldn't ask you," declared Susan. "As for me, I'd carry the flag for them."

"That would be very stupid of you," retorted her friend.

Susan was hurt. "What's stupid about it? Just watch your tongue, Jessie Paterson; it's done enough harm in the past."

She had touched a tender spot, for Jessie still felt guilty about Mr. Drummond's illness.

"You needn't remind me. It's unkind of you, Susan."

Her friend patted her knuckly hand with her plump one.

"Sorry, hen. I wouldn't hurt you for the world."

Jessie gave in with a shrug of her shoulders. "It's all right. Just keep off the subject, that's all. And off that other subject, too."

With that, they settled down to watch television.

Meanwhile, Cathy had opened her letter. On first reading, she was deeply touched. Neil needed a friend; he was anxious to see her again. Why not? asked her heart. But, using her head, she decided it would not do. What did he think she was, to play second fiddle to his fiancée? She couldn't do it; her feelings were too deeply involved. To forget about him was the only way.

"Dear Mr. Drummond," she wrote. "I accept

your apology. I'm sorry I can't be the kind of friend you want, so there is no point in us meeting again. Yours, Cathy Paton."

She gave the note to Susan and then went straight to bed, to weep into her pillow.

CHAPTER FIVE

WHEN SUSAN BRODIE got back to Airlie House after her visit to Jessie Paterson, she knocked at the sitting room door and peeped in. Evelyn Drummond was alone, her head bent over a book. She looked up with a nervous start.

"It's you, Susan. Have you had a pleasant evening?"

"Yes, thank you." She stood hesitant. "I thought Mr. Neil might be here."

"He's upstairs. Preparing a lecture, no doubt. Is it important?"

"Well, I've got a letter for him."

It was not in Evelyn's nature to pry into other people's business, even her son's, so she merely replied—

"In that case, I don't think he'll mind being interrupted."

"Right, thank you," and Susan made her way upstairs. To save electricity was of prime importance in that house, and the landing was wrapped in gloom. She tapped at Neil's door, the letter in her hand, and waited. Unseen by her, old Mrs. Drummond, whose hearing was still good, peered out of her room into the shadows.

"Who's there?" she demanded in her penetrating voice.

Susan's heart fell. "It's me."

The old lady crossed over. "What do you want with Mr. Neil?"

Susan, tempted to state that it was none of her business, thought better of it. "I've got a message for him," she said.

The other had spied the white envelope. "Not from Jessie Paterson, surely?" She knew where Susan had been. Very little passed her by that had to do with Airlie House and its occupants.

"No, it's not from her," snapped the housekeeper.

"Then it's from her niece. What can that hussy want with him?" Suppressing her anger, Susan replied—

"Cathy had an accident; you knew that. Mr. Neil wanted to know how she was, that's all."

"Indeed!" At which point Neil opened his door and put a hand out for the letter.

"Thank you, Susan, you're a good friend." Then he caught sight of his grandmother. "Not in bed yet, Grandmamma?"

"Just going." As Susan scuttled off, the old woman came closer. "Is this a secret correspondence that's going on?"

Used as he was to parrying her inquisitive remarks, he laughed teasingly—"Wouldn't you just like to know?"

"Don't put me off! This is serious. I've warned you, Neil. If you get entangled with this girl—"

"There's no question of entanglement, Gran. Now, please be good and go to bed."

"You speak to me as if I were a child!"

Patiently—"No, it is you who treat me as a child. I'm a big boy now, Gran. Goodnight to you. Pleasant dreams!" And he gently closed the door.

In his room, he quickly tore open the envelope. But it was not the message he had hoped for. Incredulous, he stared at Cathy's small, neat handwriting. "Sorry I can't be the kind of friend you want . . . No point in us meeting again—"

He simply could not believe she could be so cruel. Surely a stolen kiss did not merit such punishment? He had been mistaken in her. A prim Victorian Miss, that's what she was, and he had thought her so free and natural!

He stood transfixed, to recover from the blow. Then suddenly jerking to life, he tore the note into tiny fragments and pitched them into the wastebasket.

"There! That finishes that. I was wrong to waste a thought on her. I ought to have learned my lesson last time. From now on, it's going to be work and nothing but work!"

With this resolution, he went back to his book on marine biology, a splendid manual, which, however, he had found above the heads of his younger students. There was room for a simple textbook on the subject. Some day he might write one himself. Yes, that would be something to occupy his mind, leaving no room for regrets and vain imaginings. Girls were a waste of time. Time that could be used to better purpose.

With spring advancing, Jessie Paterson noted

with regret that her niece seemed to have lost the high spirits that had so lightened the days of winter. Instead of greeting the morning with a song, she was apt to turn over and go to sleep again. When she did burst into song, it was often cut short in midair, as if she hadn't the heart to go on. Jessie decided that she needed a tonic, but Cathy declared it was unnecessary; she was perfectly well. This was true enough, but something had gone out of life. In other words, she was eating her heart out.

It might have been better, she told herself, if Neil Drummond had lived at the other end of town, anywhere but across the Square. The sight of Airlie House from her window was enough to set hopes and fears shooting up and down.

"Perhaps I'll see him today," she would think and then take herself to task. What good would it do? It would only turn the knife in the wound. Yet she continued to look out for him and sometimes was rewarded by a sight of him setting out in the morning or perhaps returning in the evening, rather late and obviously preoccupied.

Then one day on looking out from her room to the backyard, she realized that the side window of Airlie House was just opposite and that Neil was sitting there, very still and absorbed. Not that he could see her, poised strategically behind the nylon curtains. Was that his study, then? From that moment, the knowledge gave her no peace. The only way to keep herself from looking out was to pull down the blind.

Even her work at the Medical Center lacked the sense of fulfillment these days. Patients were more difficult, the atmosphere heavy with complaint. It wasn't the patients, though, but herself. She would have to snap out of it; either that or leave the place altogether.

She was feeling at her lowest one lunchtime after completing a forenoon shift. As she entered her aunt's shop, Jessie's telltale nose indicated that something unexpected had happened.

"We've got a visitor," she proclaimed. "He telephoned early and a good thing, too. Gave me a chance to get something from the butcher."

Puzzled—"Who is it, Auntie?"

"Your father, of course. He came specially to talk to you. Don't ask me what about, for I don't know. He's upstairs."

"Good!" She was longing to see her father. She had not been home since they had parted on strained terms. Her departure had angered him, and his letters had been stiff. Now, here was a chance to make friends again.

He was in the living room, looking older, his face gray and furrowed. But his smile flashed out as she ran to kiss him.

"Dad, oh Dad! It's been a long time!"

"Too long." He patted her shoulder fondly. "How are you, Cathy? Got over that accident you had?"

"Oh, that was nothing. I'm quite agile again. I wish I had known you were coming, Dad."

"It was a sudden decision. We'll have a

talk later, you and I."

"Of course. Aunt Jessie's on her way up."

At that, Jessie appeared to put the finishing touches to the meal while Cathy set the table. During lunch, Dr. Paton brought her up to date on happenings in Kilgower and she could not prevent a feeling of nostalgia as she listened. Then, when Jessie had gone down to open the shop, he revealed the real reason for his visit.

"I was going to write you, Cathy, and then I thought I could explain better face to face. The fact is that your mother and I want you to come home."

His eyes were pleading. "Are you sure? She made it so clear that she'd be happier if I left."

"Not really. She is sorry now if she was to blame for driving you away. She would like you to forgive and forget."

"I have already forgiven and forgotten, Dad. You can tell her that."

He looked relieved. "Good. Then you'll come home?"

"That," she replied, "is quite a different matter. I am settled here, Dad, and am quite happy. Aunt Jessie likes my company."

"But that's just what I miss these days, Cathy! You were always so gay and light-hearted."

Lighthearted? She certainly had not been feeling that way lately.

"But you have my stepmother for company."

"Yes, but I need you both. I think you could pull together with a little come-and-go on both sides. There's plenty for you to do. I badly need a secretary. You could see to that side of things. There's no need for you to clash."

He was going too fast. "No, please, Dad, don't try to persuade me! I've got my job here. They depend on me."

"Your job here could be filled quite easily, but there's a big gap in Kilgower which only you can fill. Not only do I miss you, but all the folk do. The choir's not the same, for one thing. Remember the song fests and dances and all the fun you used to have?"

Yes, she remembered. Time had flown past so quickly in those days! She was missing the fun, the old friendships, the sight and sound of the sea. Perhaps Dad's new wife really meant well. If so, it might not be so bad.

Also, she would be away from the torment of being in love with a man who was not for her. Out of sight, out of mind.

Seeing the first signs of hesitation, her father urged—

"For my sake, Cathy!"

She had to turn away from his pleading gaze or she would have given in there and then.

"I can't make a decision till I've thought about it," she said at last. "It involves my whole future. I'm sure you understand."

"Of course, but don't keep me waiting too long. I'll have to leave early in the morning. Will you give me an answer before I go?"

"I'll try, but I can't promise. There are pros and cons to be weighed up, you've no idea—" and she managed to summon up a smile.

Those pros and cons kept her awake half the

night, and in the morning her mind was as confused as ever. Whatever she did would be so final! Once back in Kilgower, she would never return to Nethershaw; her job would be lost, the last chance of getting together with Neil Drummond gone for ever. On the other hand, it might be better so, and at least she would be among people she knew in a place she loved.

Joining her father and Jessie for an early breakfast, Cathy had little appetite. By this time her aunt knew what was in the wind. She refused to give advice. Though she would miss her niece very much, it was for her to decide.

"Don't be in a hurry," was her comment. "You know your failing! This is not a thing to lunge at."

Cathy agreed. "I'll write to you in a day or two, Dad. I'm afraid you'll have to be content with that."

At the station where she escorted him before going to work, she said farewell.

"Give my love to Kilgower and all my friends. It's lovely to have seen you again!"

"And lovely for me to have seen you," he replied, kissing her. "Remember, to have you near me would make me very happy."

The train slid out and Cathy turned away, her eyes dim. Walking back to the Medical Center she was still torn by indecision. In a situation like this, fate ought to take a hand, give one a pointer to show the way. Perhaps fate would be kind enough to do so? She would wait and see.

It was still early, and the only other arrival at the Center was Hilda Baxter—dutiful, conscientious Hilda. Recently there had been few confidences between these two, for in her present mood, Cathy's outgoing nature had crept into itself.

Hilda was in the small kitchen making coffee. Sometimes a doctor who had been called out in the night, was only too glad for the sustenance. This morning it was Cathy who looked as if she could do with it. Hilda offered her a cup.

"There! Sit down and drink that. You've got something on your mind. Tell me about it. You'll feel better."

"Thanks, Hilda." Perched on a rickety stool, she sipped the coffee gratefully. "I didn't sleep very well last night. Had an unexpected visit from my Dad. I've just been seeing him off. He wants me to go back home, Hilda."

Surprised, Hilda said, "Well, that's a poser. And what have you decided?"

"Nothing yet. I need someone to tell me what to do," and she looked at her expectantly.

Hilda took her time before replying. "Doesn't your heart tell you? My guess is that it prompts you to stay on here. Reason, Neil Drummond. Am I right?"

Cathy's color flared. "But he is the reason I'm tempted to leave! You know Celia Carr, don't you, Hilda?"

"Certainly I do. The family lives near us. My mother and her's are friends. She was engaged to Neil once, but it came to nothing."

"Well, it appears it's coming to something now."

Hilda was puzzled. "How do you know this?"

"She told me herself. I'd hardly have believed it from anyone else."

"Oh well, if she told you. I'm terribly sorry, Cathy!"

"I'll get over it." She slid off the stool to rinse out her coffee cup. "But going away might make it easier, don't you think?"

"Probably. You poor lamb," and she gave her arm a squeeze as they went through to reception to start the day's work.

Hilda, however, was still puzzled. She had known Celia Carr from her childhood. Always she had been the kind of girl to let nothing stand in the way of getting what she wanted. She would even tell lies. Had she fibbed to Cathy about her prospects with Neil? It was possible, though difficult to prove.

No time to ponder over it now, however. The onslaught had begun with patients and doctors arriving, telephones ringing, medical cards searched for, appointments arranged. It was lunchtime before Hilda had time to switch her mind to personal matters.

Taking leave of Cathy, she made her way to the bus stop. There was a real estate agent's window here that she often looked into. Her dreams of a house of her own always sprang to life when she studied the advertisements and photographs displayed.

Hilda had no grand aspirations. All she wanted was a place she could make into a home for herself, her man, and later a family. Four years ago when she became engaged to Charles, it had seemed within her grasp, but the hope was now receding.

As she gazed into the window, her eye was riveted by a photograph of the very house of her dreams. Just a cottage in an old-fashioned garden: two windows on the ground floor, two smaller windows above, situated on the green edge of the town.

Her heart ached with longing. Then she felt a hand on her elbow and the voice of Charles himself. It was his lunch hour, and he was making for the nearby snack bar.

"Hello," he greeted her briskly. "Off for the day, are you?" Charles was under the impression that she had a cushy job at the Center. If he only knew!

"Look at this, Charles. Roseburn Cottage is for sale. I don't suppose—"

He laughed. "You're quite right not to suppose. They'll want a fortune for that house."

"Yes, I daresay. But I've got my savings, Charles. Together we could put down something, take out a mortgage."

"Out of the question, Hilda! I've told you before, when we buy, it will be outright. We're not starting off with a yoke round our necks."

"Lots of people do," she suggested.

"But you and I have got more sense. What's wrong with things as they are? We've got good jobs, we are able to save, and we can see each other as often as we like."

"Yes," she faltered, "but we're not together. We can't have a family."

He patted her shoulder. "Time enough for that. Have a bit of patience, girl! Here's your bus, now. I'll call for you tomorrow as usual. Cheerio!"

He hurried away without even waving to her as she stood on the bus step. That was Charles. Presenting a calm face to her fellow passengers, she felt all the time as if she were weeping inside. Love shouldn't be like this. It ought to bring joy and hope.

She wasn't the only one to have her hopes dashed, however. Poor Cathy, so young and vulnerable, must have suffered deeply. Was it really a fact that Celia and Neil had come together again? She did not trust Celia and felt that she must find out the truth somehow.

Reaching the converted villa, which was home, she sat down to eat the meal which had been kept warm for her while her mother drank a cup of tea. The two, though never demonstrative, got on well with each other, and there were few secrets between them.

"What are you doing this afternoon, Mom? Bridge again?"

"I wonder how you guessed."

"It generally is," laughed Hilda. "Which of the gang is hostess this time?"

Mrs. Baxter protested: "It's a club, not a gang. It's at Mrs. Carr's today."

It seemed to be a heaven-sent chance. "Mom, will you do something for me? Find out if Celia

Carr is friendly with Neil Drummond again."

"Celia and Neil? It's the first I've heard of it. Her mother hasn't said a word to me."

"Then make sure, please. It's important."

"I'll do my best," she promised, and sure enough, when she came back after the game, she was primed with information.

"Whoever told you that Celia was on with Neil Drummond again was just blathering, Hilda. Her mother hasn't seen hide nor hair of him since one day at church, and he never even spoke to her. If they had made it up, Celia would have shouted it from the housetops, believe me!"

"You're right, Mom. Well, I'm glad and thank you very much."

"It can't be that you want Neil for yourself?" teased her mother.

"Me? I've got Charles."

"Yes, of course, Charles." She had never taken to her prospective son-in-law. He wasn't good enough for Hilda. "He's keeping you waiting too long, you know. After all, you're in your thirties."

"Don't I know it!" she declared.

However, if she could not hasten her own romance, she might now be able to give comfort to her friend.

The two girls met next morning on the way to work and walked on together.

"Have you made your decision yet, Cathy?"

"I have not," was the rueful reply. "It's with me all the time, this feeling of 'to be or not to be.' Usually I can make up my mind promptly—

too promptly, Aunt Jessie says! Were you ever faced with a fateful decision, Hilda?"

"No, but I can see it coming some day soon." She linked her arm through hers. "I've got good news for you, Cathy. My mother has been speaking to Mrs. Carr. It appears that Celia may have been lying about Neil Drummond and herself."

"Surely she wouldn't do a thing like that!"

"Wouldn't she? You don't know Celia. Not that she would consider it a real lie, just a little white one. Anyhow, Mrs. Carr is sure there's nothing in it. Neil never comes near them, never phones or writes. She would know if he did."

"I suppose so," reflected Cathy. "But Celia visits the Drummonds. I saw her coming down the steps. During the day, it was."

"When Neil wasn't at home? She'd be making up to his parents, getting a foot in the door. Leave it to Celia."

"I can hardly believe it of her."

"Well, I can. You're so fresh and innocent yourself, you think the best of everybody. That's all right, go on doing it, but beware of folk like Celia. Think it over, Cathy. Neil might be waiting for you to make a move. If you were to go away and miss the chance, you'd never forgive yourself!"

By this time they had reached the Center, where action had already begun so there was no chance for further discussion. Cathy had to steel herself to dismiss all disturbing thoughts in order to keep a clear head, but once she was back in the flat and lunch was over, she took refuge in her room to think things out.

If Celia Carr had deliberately misled her about Neil, everything would be explained, even that unexpected kiss on the landing. He had asked her for friendship and she had refused. But if there were no Celia involved, how willingly she would have given it! By this time, they might even be more than friends. Her pulse raced. She had needed a signal to make up her mind and surely this was it. She dared not leave Nethershaw as long as there was the slightest chance.

Next minute, the old, impulsive Cathy taking over, she sat down with paper and pen to let her father know that, after much thought, she had decided against coming home.

Only on the way back from posting the letter did she start to consider what was going to happen now. As for making the first move, she didn't dare. Girls in Nethershaw weren't supposed to do that sort of thing. Besides, after her curt reply to his letter, Neil would not want to have anything to do with her, probably had forgotten her by this time.

Neil had not forgotten, though he tried to believe he had. As for writing a book, he had quickly discovered that the idea was one thing, but to follow it up another. The textbook on Marine Biology wasn't coming along at all. He blamed it on the fact that he had little free time during the day, and in the evening his father and grandmother claimed his attention.

When he did escape to his study with an hour or two to spare, it was difficult to get his mind working. He would sit at his desk, chin in hand, gazing out of the window. Across the yard there was another window, nylon curtained, which he was sure was Cathy's. He had seen the curtains moving and then the blind coming down quickly. Though he shifted his desk to the other side, he still could not concentrate.

One evening, during the week after Cathy's decision to stay on in Nethershaw, he thought he would try a little music to give him inspiration. On went his radio. A Scottish dance band was playing some cheerful melodies, and shortly a singer came on the air. It was a light, happy voice; he knew one just like it. The song was a familiar one, too: "Step we gaily, on we go, heel for heel and toe for toe—" Mairi's Wedding.

Last time he heard that song, it was Cathy who sang it. The tune seemed to belong to her, so gay was it, so full of the joy of living.

When it was finished, he switched the set off and sat down at his desk, but not to write. It was weeks now since he had seen Cathy, except as a dim form behind that curtain. Was there to be a curtain between them forever? Not until this minute did he have the courage to admit the real reason for his discontent and lack of concentration.

He was in love with Cathy. This wasn't the youthful infatuation he'd had for Celia. It was a man's love, strong and deep.

"Why did I give up so easily?" he asked himself. "I ought to have followed up my plea

for friendship." She might change her mind
even yet. He must see her! Must find out if
there was any chance—

Downstairs in a jiffy, he burst into the sitting
room in a very uncharacteristic manner.

His father sat up, startled. "Is something
wrong, Neil?" His mind always ran to the
worst.

"Nothing, Dad. I'm going out. Did I hear you
say your pills were nearly finished?"

His mother put in—"There's still a few, but
probably it's time we ordered more. Perhaps
you will call in at the Medical Center? It will
be open for evening hours."

"Yes, I'll do that." He hoped he didn't sound
too willing. "Anything else?"

There was nothing, it seemed, so he let
himself out of the house, making a beeline
across the Square. He dismissed the thought
that Cathy might not be on duty. She simply
had to be!

He would know at once, when she caught
sight of him, what his fate was going to be. If
she gave him a stony stare, well, that would be
that . . . but, please don't let it be a stony stare!

There was quite a sprinkling of patients
waiting, but he wasted no glances on them.
His eyes went beyond, to the receptionists at
the long desk with the telephones and the
doctors' lights.

His heart leaped, for she was there, his
Cathy, pensive and lovely as she lent an ear to
a patient's request. Then she lifted her eyes
and saw him. What a change came over her!

Her eyes began to dance and she was smiling. Never in his life had he seen so sparkling a smile. And it was for him.

But what could he say across a desk, with eyes upon him and people crowding round?

His voice came huskily. "Will you please ask Dr. Nairn for the usual prescription for my father's pills? The name is Drummond," as if she didn't know!

"Certainly—" very businesslike as she noted it down. "Forty-eight hours to wait. The day after tomorrow."

"That will do very well." Then, desperately— "Cathy?"

But the next in line pushed in to be attended to and he had to stand aside. Cathy gave one last flicker of that smile and then was finished with him. But he wasn't finished with her, not by any means!

Unashamedly, he took his seat among the waiting patients until they all melted away. Then he approached the desk again, where Cathy was tidying up.

"Will you be going home soon?" he inquired.

"In a few minutes," she told him, the smile flickering again.

"I'd like to talk to you on the way. Any objection?"

"None at all. I'll get my things."

He waited for her at the door and they went out to the street together.

CHAPTER SIX

WHEN CATHY AND NEIL left the Medical Center, they turned by mutual consent away from the Square and started to walk westward where the sun was burnishing the hills with gold.

Here there was green countryside. Hedges were budded with young leaves and there was cherry blossom on the trees at the roadside. Cathy felt so uplifted she could not speak. Neil was silent, too. He was searching for words to heal the breach between them, though it was too soon yet to reveal his whole heart.

At length he managed to ask, unsteadily—

"Are we friends now, Cathy?"

She nodded, giving him a glowing smile. "Yes, if you still want that, Neil."

"I do, very much. That note you sent by Susan Brodie seemed so unlike you. What made you write it?"

Cathy hesitated before replying—"It was a misunderstanding. I—I thought you already had a girlfriend. Celia Carr."

"Celia Carr! But that was in the past. I haven't seen Celia for years, excepting once. How did you get that into your head?"

"Oh, just—" She would not betray Celia, she was too happy. "Let's forget about it, Neil."

"Of course." Then he added impulsively—"I have been missing you so much. Did you miss me?"

"Yes, I did," she admitted. "I nearly went home to my father. I'm glad now I didn't."

"So am I." Suppose she had gone, that they would never meet again? He could not bear to think of it.

After a time they stopped at the gate of a field to watch the antics of some frolicking lambs. There they were, leaping and bounding without a care.

"They look so happy, don't they?" Cathy observed.

He smiled down at her. She loved his smile; it was warm and sincere, a reflection of true feeling.

"Would you like to be like that, Cathy? Carefree, no problems, no anxieties about the future?"

"It would be very enjoyable," she reflected, "but one would miss a lot, too. I think I'd rather be human, even with problems and anxieties."

"My opinion, too. We seem to agree about a lot of things."

They spent a long time leaning over that gate exchanging confidences.

"It's rather strange that we should think alike," Cathy observed. "After all, you're a clever, serious type of person, and I am what Aunt Jessie calls 'bee headed.' "

He would not have it. "Lighthearted, rather, but you can be serious, too."

"But you have known me such a little while."

"Wrong. I seem to have known you for centuries."

"And I feel the same about you," she admitted.

"I'm glad." He pulled her around to face him, his arms tightening around her. But Cathy drew back.

"No, please. No kissing."

"But you let me, once. You liked it, don't deny it!"

"I'm not denying it. But I'd rather just be friends. When people start to kiss they become very silly sometimes."

Neil laughed out. "The things you say! But you might be right."

"I am," she said seriously. "You told me you needed a friend and I need one, too. A friend is someone to tell your troubles to and to listen to theirs. To be ready to help, if needed. To cheer each other up or just to talk about things you can't tell anyone else. I haven't put it very well, but do you agree?"

"Certainly. I couldn't have put it better myself. All right, Cathy, we'll keep it at that. As my friend, do you object if I think about you a lot, even when you're not there?"

"I'd love you to think about me," she confessed, "for I often think about you, too. Especially when I see your window from my room. You sit there studying, don't you?"

He was amazed. "I do. And sometimes I imagine you're there behind the curtain. That means we could signal to each other, couldn't we?"

The idea appealed to her romantic heart. "What fun!"

But the sun had disappeared behind a cloud, bringing them back to reality.

"Neil, we're miles from home! Your folks will be worried."

"I suppose so," he agreed unwillingly. "Shall we go back?"

They turned toward town again, still wrapped up in each other. They passed a few people whom Cathy knew by sight.

"A pity," she told him. "It's such a gossipy place this! I'd rather no one knew we were friends."

"Why shouldn't they know?" he demanded. "I'd like you to come to Airlie House soon and get properly acquainted with my people. You'd love my mother. Dad is more difficult but all right at heart. As for my Gran—well, she's the strong-minded sort. You've got to stand up to her."

"Which I couldn't possibly do," murmured Cathy. "I'm sorry, Neil, but could it be just you and me in the meantime?"

The certain disapproval of his family would just ruin things at the outset. Whatever happened in the future, this precious moment must be kept unspoiled.

"As you wish, Cathy, but there can't be many secrets in a town like this. What about your Aunt; won't you tell her?"

She smiled. "Aunt Jessie practically ordered me to have nothing to do with you."

"I see. That silly feud. I only had my grandmother's version of that."

"And I've only had Aunt Jessie's, which is bound to be one-sided. It all happened just before I came here. Your father's business was flourishing then. He was keen on buying up property and modernizing it. He had set his mind on acquiring Aunt Jessie's shop."

"So I gathered. She refused to sell to him."

"She would neither sell nor allow it to be modernized. Perhaps she was wrong, I don't know. Your father called the shop a blot on the landscape and she never forgave him. She said her shop would be there long after his jerry-built buildings had collapsed. They had a fine set-to! Aunt Jessie can be awful when she's roused."

"So can my father, I'm afraid."

"The worst of it was that your father became ill and your Gran blames Aunt Jessie. I don't think your mother does. Aunt Jessie likes her, Neil. Nobody could help liking her."

"You're right, Cathy. Poor Mom, she's not very happy, I'm afraid. That's partly why I came home. It was a big decision to make."

"Tell me about it."

It was the first time he had revealed to anyone the mental battle he had gone through at the time.

"In the States I was my own man, responsible to no one except those I worked for. The prospects were dazzling, Cathy."

"Yet you gave them up to come back and be tied to home life again."

"Yes. Though I love Scotland and I love my home, don't doubt that. But the ties of affection do make for a kind of imprisonment. One is no longer free."

She knew exactly what he meant. "Yet who would be without ties of affection? We might as well be zombies."

So they talked on without restraint until, having reached the Square, they stopped to say goodnight. They had not meant to linger, but it seemed impossible to tear themselves apart. The May night was warm and still, daytime traffic had ceased, and the street was deserted.

"I'll call for you again tomorrow night, same time," he told her.

She smiled. "So soon?"

"There's a poem that says—'Gather ye rose-buds while ye may, Old time is still a-flying.' Let's grasp the moment, Cathy."

"I'm all in favor," was the reply.

Their hands touched, and she sped lightly away while he walked with more thoughtful tread toward his home.

Cathy had no key to the flat and was obliged to ring the bell. Aunt Jessie opened the door, her face a big question mark.

"Well! You had me worried. If you'd just told me you'd be late—"

"I didn't know. There was lots of work to do tonight."

Jessie eyed her severely. "Cathy, don't pretend. That place has been locked up for more than an hour; I've got eyes! However, I don't wish to pry into your affairs. If you don't want to tell me, you needn't!" and she flounced away.

In this mood Jessie could keep a huffed silence for long enough, making things very uncomfortable. Cathy followed her into the room, slipping her arm through her aunt's.

"Don't be angry, Auntie, please! I just met somebody and got talking."

Jessie noted the heightened color, the light in her eye.

"Ay, I can guess who the somebody was! And me thinking that affair had fizzled out."

"It wasn't an affair and it still isn't. We're just friends, Aunt Jessie, and I'm so happy!"

Jessie shook her head at her. "It always starts with 'just friends.' It's not in the nature of things to stay like that. Anyhow, you can't be friends without his people knowing about it."

"Perhaps you can help us there," suggested her niece.

"I'll do no such thing. No, Cathy, I'll not hinder you, but I shan't help either, and that's that."

Even this verdict did not lessen her spirits, however. She went singing into her room to take off her things. It was dusk now and she switched on the light.

At the same time a light went on in the window opposite. He was there! She could see him outlined against the glass, and she waved energetically. Neil was not slow to reply. Wonderful! They had established a link that nobody could spoil, neither Aunt Jessie, his parents, or his fierce old grandmother. It was their own secret. Her romantic heart was satisfied.

Up in her room, old Mrs. Drummond was waiting impatiently for her grandson's return. Had he forgotten that this was the night they played Scrabble together? Evelyn had told her that Neil had gone out to order a new prescription for his father, but that was a long time ago. Soon it would be too late. She liked to go to bed early, get the best of the night before the dawn chorus started in the Square gardens, to be followed inexorably by the noise of traffic. She hardly ever got a full night's sleep, the penalty of growing old.

She'd found that a pleasant game of Scrabble helped her to relax. Also, she was good at the game, often beating Neil, the brilliant scholar. It gave a boost to her ego. There she sat at the card table with the board set out, ready to begin, but no Neil. Not much use playing by herself! It was most unlike him to forget; something must have detained him. Not an accident, she hoped.

Frustrated, she was about to close up the board when she heard his footstep on the stair. Home at last. Well, if he had an excuse she would forgive him, but it would have to be good.

She waited for his knock at the door, his cheery greeting, but it did not come. Was it possible he had gone to his own room, forgotten all about her?

It took her some time to get up from her chair and hobble out to the landing. His door was half open and she looked in. The light was on, and there was Neil at the window waving to somebody in the flat across the yard. No mystery as to who it was. That girl Cathy, Jessie Paterson's niece.

So it had come to that. He'd been out with her; she was more important to him than his own grandmother. Standing there in the doorway, she gave a sharp little cough and he turned around. He did not even look ashamed of himself!

"Hello, Gran, do you need me?"

"Need you! Did you forget it was our Scrabble night?"

Oh, dear. She set such store by that game. He was truly sorry.

"It did slip my mind, Gran, but it's not too late. Let's have a game now."

"I don't feel in the mood for it now," she replied stiffly. "I'm too tired. And worried."

"I'm sorry. What's worrying you?"

"You know perfectly well. You were waving to that girl."

Though annoyed with her, he passed this off with a laugh.

"There's no law against waving to a girl, Gran. In any case, it really has nothing to do with you, has it?"

So, insult added to injury. She drew herself up.

"I thought I had some say in this house!"

"Nobody denies that; but no say in how I choose my friends. Come on, let me take you back to your room."

She threw off his helping hand. "No thanks, I prefer to go alone."

In an attempt to pacify her, he said, "Very well. We'll have a game of Scrabble soon."

"Tomorrow?" she asked edgily.

"I'm afraid not. I'm doing something else tomorrow."

"I see. Well, it doesn't matter. Don't bother about Scrabble in the future. I've lost the notion for it," and she walked out, head erect.

Cathy had pulled down her blind, so he did the same. He was sorry they had been caught. Gran was really a very naughty old lady, but she could not do any harm to their friendship, however much she disapproved.

Sitting down at his desk, he read over the notes he had made for the textbook he was planning. Yes, he could see his way now; the urge was on him again. That was because of his talk with Cathy. To have her to confide in was going to make all the difference in his life.

In the Medical Center consulting hours were over, and Cathy and Hilda, still on late duty, were left to tidy up and get ready for next day. Forgotten umbrellas and parcels were stowed away to be called for, they hoped, by the owners. The cards of patients who had made appointments were extracted from the filing cabinet, forms filled out, other clerical duties completed.

At last Cathy found time to ask her friend—

"Is Charles coming to meet you tonight?"

"He is not," replied Hilda. "He rang to say his mother needs him at home to do some painting. She's the house-proud sort. I hope he doesn't expect me to be the same!"

"One can be proud of a house without being house-proud," observed Cathy.

"I agree. Cathy, I've seen a house I could be proud of. Roseburn Cottage is up for sale. I was keen to buy it, but Charles wants to wait till we've got more money."

"You've waited long enough! It's not fair, Hilda. Any sensible man would have snapped you up long ago. Charles doesn't appreciate you. You're a girl in a thousand. Dr. Nairn thinks so, anyway."

"Because I'm useful to him. I suppose it's something, to be of use," she mused. "I'm certainly not ornamental."

"Well, I think you are better than ornamental. Charles takes you for granted, Hilda. Give him a fright. Go out with someone else for a change."

The other looked shocked. "I'd never dream of it! Besides, who is there to go out with? I'm getting on, you know."

"Nonsense! You're as old or as young as you feel." Cathy closed a drawer with a click and turned to her friend, who was eyeing her speculatively.

"You're looking pretty young yourself, today. There's something different about you, Cathy. That sparkle in your eye. Has it worked out with Neil Drummond, then?"

She nodded happily. "He's calling for me tonight. In fact, here he is now."

She went to open the glass door through which Neil was peering.

"Come on in! There's only Hilda and me. We're ready to leave."

Neil's car was at the curb. Hilda gratefully accepted his offer to run her home. The journey to her house at the other end of the town took only a few minutes. As they stopped to let Hilda off at her gate, a girl came out of a nearby house and passed close by, inspecting the occupants of the car. Neil did not see her, but Cathy did.

"That," she observed as they started off again, "was Celia Carr."

He did not seem interested. "I had forgotten Celia lived in this part of the town."

"She saw us, Neil."

"Why shouldn't she? I want people to see you with me. Oh, I know what you're going to say: my parents will get to hear. All the better if they do. Why won't you come and meet them, Cathy?"

"I told you; it would spoil everything. We've got to bide our time. Where are you taking me, Neil?"

"Loch Creenan, of course. Unless you've another preference."

"Not at all. I didn't see it properly last time. The day you rescued me, remember?"

He smiled reminiscently. "Very clearly. I also remember that first time, when you came a cropper on top of the milk bottles."

"I don't do that sort of thing any more," she assured him. "I've stopped 'lunging.' I'm growing up."

"Sorry about that. Please don't become too

staid and sober! You wouldn't be Cathy if you
did." And he turned uphill toward the solitude
of the loch.

At the edge of the water, he stopped the car.
The surface was still and beautiful under the
evening sky. The greening trees came right
down to the brink in some parts, their shadows
reflected below. One or two small islands dotted
the surface. They looked like fairy isles, out of
this world.

"It's very beautiful," she sighed.

"Beautiful, but that's not all. These waters
can be beneficial as well, if put to fish farming."

"But," she objected, "wouldn't that spoil the
beauty?"

"It needn't. Have you ever seen Loch Faskally
at Pitlochry? I'll take you there someday and
you'll see."

That started him on his favorite subject, and
soon he was telling her about his studies,
analyzing the plankton netted from the loch to
find out if it contained the proper nutrients.

Cathy listened carefully, not only because he
was Neil but because she was truly interested.
When he told her about his projected book, she
felt an added thrill.

"I'm so glad you're telling me all this."

"You're a good listener, that's why. Somehow,
I knew you would be. But you must let me
know if I begin to bore you."

"You could never bore me!"

When at last they took the homeward way
and he stopped at the entrance to Aunt Jessie's
flat, they again felt a reluctance to part.

"I do wish you would come up and see Aunt Jessie!"

"But she doesn't approve of me."

"She would, if she knew you. Her bark is worse than her bite. I think," she added confidently, "I can handle Aunt Jessie."

"Some relations do take a lot of handling. My grandmother, for instance," he observed grimly. "But if you really wish it, I'll come up and have a chat. Her heart might melt; you never know."

They left the car and as they mounted the stairs, he reminded her: "Last time I carried you up, and at the top—"

"We'll forget about that, if you don't mind," said Cathy as she rang the bell.

Aunt Jessie opened the door. She looked startled and not a little annoyed.

"Cathy, I thought I told you—"

"Yes, you did, but please invite Neil in! He'll go away if you don't and I want him to stay."

Seeing there was no choice, Jessie stood aside.

"Come in then, Mr. Drummond. But I might as well warn you, I've got a visitor."

Neil hesitated, while Cathy asked—"Who is it?"

"Susan Brodie," she was informed.

At that, Susan herself peeped into the hall. "It's yourself, Mr. Neil!"

Neil hesitated no longer. He knew their secret was safe with the trusty housekeeper who had shared many of his confidences in the past.

After that, the evening became very lively indeed. Recalling the gathering in the kitchen at Airlie House, Susan insisted that Cathy should sing to them. There was a piano of sorts in the room and Neil found himself seated there, accompanying the songs. He was not much of a pianist and some of the notes were sour, but Cathy's voice and high spirits carried them along.

Eventually, they all joined in. Susan had a hearty soprano, Jessie a rather croaky contralto, and Neil's voice was a pleasant baritone. They found an old copy of *The Scottish Students' Song Book,* full of every variety of ditty, from which they chose such numbers as "Over the Sea to Skye," some tuneful folk melodies such as "Danny Boy," and ended up with the universal favorite "My Bonnie Lies Over the Ocean."

By this time, refreshment was called for, and Jessie made a cup of tea. Sitting round the table, laughing and talking, everybody forgot the time until Susan looked at the clock and exclaimed:

"Mercy me! I'll be nodding all day tomorrow!"

"Me, too," said Neil, laughing. "I'll run you round, Susan."

To Cathy at the door, he said—"I'll phone you. May I, Aunt Jessie?"

By this time, Jessie was in a very good humor.

"You'll do what you like, you two, whatever I say."

He grinned at Cathy. "That's right. Come

along, Susan," and he took her plump arm to lead her down the stairs.

"I'll slip in by the back door," she said, as he drove round to the garage. "That was rare good fun, Mr. Neil. Yon Cathy's a fine lass, genuine through and through."

"My opinion, too," he agreed, with feeling.

He unlocked the front door and went in. There was a light in the sitting room, so they must still be up, excepting his grandmother, no doubt.

But, on looking in, he saw that the old lady was there with his parents, sitting at the dying fire. There was a tension in the atmosphere, which he felt the moment he stepped into the room.

"Hello, there, I hope I haven't kept you out of bed," he began cheerfully.

His mother was the only one who smiled. "We weren't sure if you had your key, Neil, but now you're here, we can make a move."

She folded up her knitting and went to help her husband rise. But Mr. Drummond sat on stiffly, his brows contracting as he regarded his son. His muffled words came accusingly—

"We don't seem to get much of your company these days, Neil!"

The unfair accusation stung him to the quick.

"Sorry, Dad, but you know how busy I am. One needs a little relaxation!"

"And being with your family is a task. I see."

Neil swallowed. Dad was not well. He must be patient.

"You know I don't think that! Otherwise, would I have chosen to come home at all?"

His mother took his arm placatingly. "We are only too glad you did come home, Neil."

"Thank you, Mom."

His grandmother had not yet spoken. She just sat there, stern mouth compressed.

"Can I help you upstairs, Gran?" he offered.

"Get me out of the way, you mean? No, I'm staying here. We'll have this out," she declared.

"I don't understand."

"Of course you do. We had a visit tonight from an old friend of yours, Celia Carr."

"Really." He turned from one to the other. "How does that affect me?"

"She calls sometimes to see your father," Evelyn Drummond explained. "He quite enjoys her company."

"Yes," the old lady put in, "and tonight she just happened to mention she had seen you on her way here."

He was beginning to understand. "Well, I didn't happen to see her. What of it?"

"No wonder you didn't see her. You were with Jessie Paterson's niece again. I have just been telling your parents about what happened last night. It's only right they should know."

He gave her glance for glance. "I'm sorry you took it on yourself to do that, but if you hadn't, I should have told them myself pretty soon."

His father's hands had tightened on the arms of his chair.

"So," he stuttered, "it's true, then. You knew

how things were between me and that—that woman Paterson, and yet you—you deliberately take up with this niece of hers!"

"And why not?" Neil kept his voice cool. "Your quarrels are your own affair, Dad. In any case, you should surely let bygones be bygones."

"Never!" declared the other. "That woman is impossible. She said crude, unforgivable things. No doubt this—this upstart of a girl is the same type—"

This time, Neil lost his calm. "You will please take that back, Dad! Cathy is no upstart. She is the sweetest, kindest—" his voice failed.

"You have lost your senses, Neil," said his grandmother. "Next thing we know, you'll be asking her to marry you."

He faced her squarely—"That," he declared, "is exactly what I intend to do."

"No!" His father had staggered to his feet. "You can't! If you must marry, let it be—be somebody in your own position, that we can be proud of. Think of your education, your career."

"Cathy is the one to help me with that," he said stubbornly. "Come on, Dad, be reasonable. It is my choice, not yours, whom I marry."

He was holding his father's arm, to steady him.

Then, his voice coming in gasps, Mr. Drummond made his response.

"If you go against me in this, Neil, you are no son of mine!"

With that, he suddenly went limp. Neil caught him as he fell to the floor. He bore his father across to the sofa and laid him there, inert and speechless, while his wife ran to his side. Then old Mrs. Drummond rose and limped to the telephone.

"I'll ring the doctor." And to Neil, in scathing tones, she screeched, "Now you see the harm you've done!"

CHAPTER SEVEN

CHANGED DAYS, mused Jessie Paterson as she sorted out her newspapers in the shop next morning. There was Cathy upstairs, singing like a bird just as she used to do. All seemed well now between her and Neil Drummond. That Neil was in love with her, Jessie had no longer any doubt. That he would marry her seemed less sure. The opposition of his family would certainly complicate matters. Was Neil strong enough to go his own way, and if they did marry against his parents' wishes, what kind of life could Cathy expect to have?

All ready for an early start at the Medical Center, her niece came running downstairs to say goodbye. She made a colorful picture in her cherry red jumper, shining hair, and blue eyes sparkling with the joy of living.

"Happy?" inquired Jessie, but there was no need to ask.

"On top of the world," was the gay reply.

At that moment the phone rang, cutting off her blithe assurance.

"I'll take it, Auntie! It will be Neil."

"As early as this? I don't believe it."

But it was Neil. There was a note in his voice that dimmed Cathy's smile.

"Good morning, Cathy. I'm glad I got you before you left."

"So am I!"

"It's bad news, I'm afraid."

She caught her breath. "Oh, Neil, what is it?"

"My father took a bad turn last night. He is in the hospital."

Coming down with a shock from the heights of her dream world, she said shakily—

"I'm terribly sorry. Is it—is it serious?"

"We don't know yet, but I'm afraid it is. I thought I'd better let you know. You'll understand if you don't hear from me? My mother is in a state—"

"Of course I understand! Put me out of your mind, Neil; do your best for them. Is there anything I can do to help?"

His voice husky, he replied, "Nothing, Cathy, but thanks for asking. I'll get in touch with you as soon as I can. Goodbye for now!"

Putting down the receiver, she turned a stricken face to her aunt.

"His father is in the hospital. He took ill last night."

"Bad sign," murmured Jessie. "Just when you were so happy. It so often happens."

"Perhaps it isn't so bad," Cathy hoped. "But I'm sorry for Neil. His mother, too. She's had a lot of trouble. But I'd better be off, Auntie. Doctors and patients will be chomping at the bit. Good thing it's Saturday, with a free afternoon."

In the street everything was going on as

usual. Up there, Airlie House was looking just
the same, with nothing to indicate what had
happened there last night.

According to Neil, his father's health had
been improving of late; they had not expected
a relapse. There must be a reason for it. That
the reason had anything to do with herself,
Cathy did not for a moment suspect. She only
knew that the day was less bright than it had
been an hour ago.

She had awakened with a song in her heart,
but now she did not feel in the least like
singing.

On Saturday afternoons Jessie's shop was
usually overrun with children spending their
pocket money on comics or candy. If they did
not behave, she could be as nippy with them as
with her adult customers, but they all knew
her bark was worse than her bite. Though she
would stand no backtalk, she was ready to give
sympathy and an extra sweet where it was
due.

It worried her to think how little the kids
got for their money nowadays. When she was a
child, you could get a lot of candy for a penny;
just about what you got for five today. She still
thought in terms of pennies at times. It wasn't
advisable, though; only made you pine for days
long gone.

"Come on now, Bobbie, I haven't got all day!
You'll have to learn to make quick decisions;
that's how to get on in the world. Or perhaps
you don't want to get on?"

Bobbie grinned. "I want to have a shop like yours."

"Well, I didn't get it by dithering, that's one thing sure. Come on, now—licorice or caramels, which?"

In the end he took neither, but some highly colored raspberry sweets, not nearly so good for him. As Jessie recorded the sale on her cash register, the boys went out and a tall old lady with a stick walked in. She stood inside the door, her large featured face expressing extreme distaste of her surroundings.

Jessie looked up and couldn't believe her eyes. That "Lady Drummond" should grace her humble shop with her presence was unheard of. It was obvious she had come on no pleasant errand and Jessie's sensitive nose twitched. Battle loomed ahead.

They stood gazing at each other, Jessie determined she was not going to be the first to speak. It was the other who broke the silence.

"I came to see your niece," she stated curtly. "Where is she?"

"Not here," replied Jessie, just as curtly. As a matter of fact, Cathy, having the afternoon off, was upstairs in the apartment.

"I can see that for myself. Nevertheless, I insist on seeing her."

"May I ask," Jessie inquired frostily, "what your business is with her?"

"That is for her ears. I shall wait till she comes in," and the old woman sat down on the chair beside the counter.

Jessie would have let her wait there all

afternoon, but in a few minutes Cathy herself came downstairs, ready to give a helping hand. On seeing the visitor, she stopped short, but it was too late. Mrs. Drummond tapped the floor with her stick.

"You, Cathy, whatever your name is—I want a word with you!"

"I'm afraid it's not convenient at the moment," she parried.

"Then make it convenient. Take me somewhere we can be alone."

There seemed no help for it. "If you care to come upstairs—?"

With much difficulty the old lady was hoisted up the wooden stairs which connected with the flat above. Then she sat herself down in the living room, panting a little.

"So this is where you live," she commented disparagingly.

"My aunt's flat is a good place to live. Please tell me what you came for!"

"I wish to talk to you very seriously about my grandson."

The other's color flamed. "Yes?"

"Perhaps you have heard that his father is in the hospital."

"I have. I'm sorry. Is there any word?" she asked.

"Nothing definite as yet, but he is very ill. We expected a full recovery, and now—this."

"Yes, you must be very upset. But I don't understand. What have I to do with Mr. Drummond's illness?"

Tapping sharply with her stick, she said,

"You have everything to do with it!"

Cathy still did not understand. "But, how?"

"If you had any gumption, you would know. Don't think I haven't been aware of what's going on between you and Neil."

Hotly—"There's nothing going on!"

"You are lying. You have worked on my grandson till he imagines he is in love with you."

Cathy, on her feet, was tense with indignation. "That's nonsense. We are friends, that's all."

"That is not what he says."

"What does he say, then?" she asked breathlessly.

"That he intends to marry you."

"It's the first I knew of it," she declared.

The old lady sniffed. "Don't pretend! It was what you schemed for from the start, wasn't it?"

"I didn't scheme. You are quite wrong about us. We like each other, yes, but there is nothing more."

"No? He seems to think there is. However, I am relieved to hear it isn't true. I hope it will never be, for everybody's sake. Especially his father's."

Cathy asked, though she had guessed. "Why that?"

"Because it was when Neil told him of his intentions that he had this sudden relapse. My son would never agree to this marriage. If Neil were to persist, it would be his father's death knell."

Cathy sat staring at her. Was this true? Was

she to blame, unwittingly, for what had happened?

"I can hardly believe you," she murmured through white lips.

"I am not in the habit of telling lies," was the stiff response. "I have told you the truth. If you have any finer feelings at all, you will know what to do about it."

She meant, of course, breaking off with Neil altogether. Oh yes, that would please her mightily, bitter as she was about the stand Aunt Jessie had taken against her son's plans.

"Well?" she persisted as Cathy stood there voiceless.

"Well, what?"

"I want your promise to have nothing more to do with my grandson."

"I'm sorry, but you're asking too much. There are Neil's wishes to be considered."

"Neil has lost his head, and not for the first time. He is much too impressionable. The first affair had a short life. This one will, too, if you leave him alone."

Cathy's response was deliberate. "I don't think it's for you to say. If that's all you came for, Mrs. Drummond, you needn't stay any longer."

The old lady got slowly to her feet, "It's for Neil's sake I have appealed to you. If you have any real feeling for him, you will give him up. If anything happened to his father and he felt responsible, it would blight his life." Leaning heavily on her stick she made a move to the door. Avoiding the shop, Cathy helped her out to the street. The last words came from her visitor.

"Think about it!" she commanded, as she departed without so much as another glance.

Cathy's eyes followed the stiff, limping figure. How could she help but think about it! The interview had been one she would never forget.

She returned to the flat, benumbed. Neil had given her no hint about the cause of his father's collapse. But of course he would not hurt her by doing so. Had he really intimated his intention to marry her? Her pulses started to race.

So he was in love with her after all. She hadn't been quite sure, had hoped against hope, waiting to hear it from his own lips. In spite of everything, her heart beat high. With love between them, surely they could overcome all obstacles? Love, after all, was the greatest thing in the world. Nothing should stand in its way. That was what she had always believed.

She must see Neil immediately; he was the only one who could give her the true facts. But, how was it to be done? She could not call at the house and ask to see him. Neither could she telephone, for someone else might answer. There was only one possibility. Susan Brodie was a true friend and she was always welcome in her kitchen. She would go round to the back door where no one would see her.

Aunt Jessie was busy in the shop as Cathy passed through.

"Has your visitor gone?" she turned to ask.

Cathy nodded. "I'll tell you about that later."

"She's upset you. I knew it!"

"I'm all right," Cathy assured her. "Just going out for a breath of fresh air."

"Ay, you look as if you need it!"

Indeed the cool wind was very welcome on her hot cheeks as she went through the yard at the back of Airlie House. To her relief, Susan answered her tentative knock, greeting her with her usual warmth.

Seated in the gleaming kitchen, Cathy asked—

"Have they heard any more about Mr. Drummond, Susan?"

She nodded. "Ay, they phoned the hospital a little while ago. It seems it's not so bad as they feared."

The relief was so great, tears sprang to her eyes. "Oh, thank God for that!"

Susan was surprised by the depth of her reaction. "Lassie, you don't even know the man."

"He's Neil's father," she said simply. "Susan, I'll confess why I came. I simply must see Neil. Does he happen to be at home?"

"Ay, he came in a while ago. I'll tell him you're here. *Sub rosa*, eh?"

A small smile. "Yes, Susan, secretly. I'm sorry, but it's got to be that way."

"I understand," she patted her hand. "I'll leave you two together, don't worry."

She disappeared, and in a few moments Neil was beside her, his smile flashing out in a careworn face. He took her hands and pressed them.

"How thoughtful of you to come! The news is better, Cathy. Dad will get over this attack, they say."

"Susan told me. He'll have to be careful, though."

"Oh dear, yes! Any sort of shock or worry would send him right back again."

"Then he mustn't have any worry," she declared. "You've got to shield him."

He pressed her hand to his lips. "Spoken like the wise little person you are. I'll do my best to spare him in every way."

"That's right." She stepped back from him, pleading eyes on his face, "If he knew you and I were so friendly, that would worry him, wouldn't it?"

He hesitated, asking gently—"What put that into your head, Cathy?"

"Well, I just thought that he might have heard about us and—and got so angry that it brought on his relapse."

Silent for a moment, Neil looked at her searchingly.

"Someone told you this. My grandmother went out on her own this afternoon, a thing she seldom does. Was it her, Cathy?"

Her eyes fell. She could not lie to him. "Well, yes, it was."

His smile vanished, to be replaced by an angry frown.

"What right had she to do this? I shall tell her what I think of her!"

"No, Neil, please. She mustn't know I told you. But I had to find out the truth."

"Of course you had." He put a protective arm round her. "It wasn't your fault, Cathy. Rather it was mine for being precipitate. Dad brought me to the point where I was obliged to confess that I love you and want to marry you."

Her glance met his. The tender look on his face almost broke her down. "I didn't know," she whispered.

"Do you love me, Cathy? Real love, not just friendship?"

She nodded. "Real love. Right from the start."

"Darling!" Caught up in his arms, she surrendered to his kisses. Everything was forgotten except the mutual ecstasy that transcended every other thought.

"I'll never let you go, never!" he declared, at last.

But Cathy drew away. "Neil, what are we thinking of? We mustn't give in to what we feel. Everything is against it."

He kissed her again, intensely. "There's nothing against it, nothing! I love you and you love me, that's all that matters."

Sadly, she shook her head. "No, Neil. There is a gap between us that cannot be bridged—not now, not even by the power of our love."

He frowned. "That's my grandmother talking through you. You shouldn't have listened to her."

"I had to. And I realize she was right."

He took her by the shoulders. "You and I belong to each other. No one is going to part us."

Near to tears, Cathy said, "We've got to part. At least till we have a chance to consider things calmly. We can't do that if we go on seeing each other. I'm not strong enough—"

she broke off, pushing him away. He stood there, hands clenched, gazing at her.

"You're right, I can't be calm when you're beside me."

"That proves my point," she maintained. "Besides, we couldn't meet without people seeing us. Your grandmother would get to know, no doubt your father, too. You must give him a chance to get well."

He took a deep breath. "I suppose you are right. The Nethershaw grapevine is pretty potent. But we live so near! The light in your window is a beacon to me. Must I stop thinking about you as well as seeing you?"

"No," she pleaded, "please do think about me! I couldn't bear it if you forgot me."

He took her in his arms again. "Impossible! You're there in my thoughts every minute."

"Even when you're lecturing and writing your book?" she teased.

"Even then. You're my inspiration. Truly, Cathy, I have done everything better since I got to know you. You've given me faith and hope. We can still hope, can't we?"

She nodded. "No harm hoping. Perhaps a way will open up." But she did not see how that could be possible.

They clung together for a long moment before saying goodbye. Then she slipped out of the back door unseen. She felt that the line she had taken was the right one. Neil himself would not have proposed it for fear of hurting her, but now he would be conscience-free, both as regarded his father and herself.

Yes, she had done the right thing, but it would be nothing less than agony for her to be so near him and yet divided by an invisible wall. If she could only get away from Nethershaw for a time! But her two-week vacation was not yet due. Hilda Baxter would be off next week, however; she might possibly exchange with her. But perhaps Hilda and Charles were going away together, no doubt accompanied by his mother as usual? No harm in making inquiries, however.

On Monday, both Hilda and Cathy were on the late shift at the Center. After even—ing hours, when they were alone, the two young women began chatting about personal affairs.

"How's Charles?" asked Cathy. "Any word of a wedding yet?"

Hilda was busy at the filing cabinet. "No, Cathy, and there's not likely to be."

"You don't mean it's all off?" Shaken out of her own preoccupation, she noticed that her friend's face was pale, her eyes shadowed. Come to think of it, Hilda had not been looking herself of late.

"Not off, exactly. I'm fighting hard at the moment."

"With Charles, you mean?"

A slight smile. "With myself, Cathy, I've been hanging on to Charles, even though I don't love him any more. I told myself love would come back after we were married, but I know him too well now."

"I see." Cathy finished some typing notes

and put them in a drawer. "You haven't told him yet?"

"It seems so final," she sighed. "I did so wish for a home and a family!"

"There are other men, Hilda."

"For me, at my age? I am not attractive to men."

"You underrate yourself," Cathy scolded her. "If I were you, I'd take the bull by the horns tonight. Otherwise you'll torment yourself out of existence. It's wrong to marry without love. But perhaps I'm not the best person to give advice. I badly need it myself!"

"But I thought everything was going well with you."

"So did I! But something has happened. I'm in a terrible dilemma, Hilda."

"You too? I'm sorry. Would you like to tell me about it?"

Cathy hesitated. "You've enough troubles of your own."

"It's only when you have troubles yourself that you understand other people's," was the reply.

Thus encouraged, Cathy launched out on her story. Hilda listened sympathetically, as she always did.

"So," Cathy finished, "I have love trouble, too. It looks as if Neil and I were fated to stay apart. He told me last night that he loved me, but there's too much at stake. It's a matter of life and death, actually. Another row with his father might be fatal. At the best, it means we'd have to wait till dear knows when—forever, perhaps."

"Yes, I can see that. And waiting isn't your strong point, is it?"

Cathy gave a short laugh. "You're right. I haven't got your angelic temperament. Besides, I'd hate to feel that Neil was bound in any way. It might be better to part altogether, go somewhere out of sight and sound of him."

"You could go back home, perhaps!" suggested the other. "Not that I'd want you to!"

"I did think of that. If I could go home for a week or two right now, see how it would work—"

Hilda seemed to guess what she was leading up to.

"If you like, I'll exchange vacations with you," she offered.

"Angel! But haven't you arranged something with Charles?"

"Oh, Charles. He was supposed to be booking up for us—and his mother, of course, for a stay in Bute, but everything is too dear, he says."

He would, thought Cathy. "Would August suit you all right?" she asked anxiously.

"Fine. I'll go somewhere on my own or with the family."

"Good. I'll be eternally indebted, Hilda."

She waited on, until Charles himself put in a belated appearance. How smug he looked, how sure of himself and of the girl to whom he was engaged!

Watching them walk away together, Cathy wondered if Hilda would have the courage to speak her mind, or drift on as she had been doing, contemplating a marriage without love for the sake of a home and family.

Nowadays, Charles and Hilda never had much to say to each other; they seemed to have said it all. They proceeded in silence until Charles, in his possessive way, took her arm to hasten her step. He felt her stiffen.

"What's up, Hilda?"

"Nothing special. I prefer to walk alone, that's all. You—you treat me as if I belonged to you."

"Don't you want to belong to me, then?" he asked in hurt surprise.

"I belong to myself," she declared. "By the way, Charles, I'm going on vacation alone this year. In August."

"But you can't do that! I've just managed to get rooms in Rothesay for the three of us. A cancellation will mean a fairly high penalty."

"I'm sorry, but it's too late. You can take your mother to Rothesay; she'll be glad to get you to herself. I've promised Cathy Paton to exchange with her."

"Then you can tell her you've changed your mind!"

"But I haven't. You've kept me hanging on too long about this vacation, Charles. And about other things, too."

"I don't know what you mean about other things," he mumbled.

"You know well enough. We're no nearer getting married than we were four years ago. Another four years and it would be the same story. So—" at last she took the plunge—"we'd better end it now."

Astonished and alarmed—"End it? You mean break our engagement?"

She turned to confront him. "Yes, Charles. The fact is, I stopped loving you some time ago."

He could not believe it. "Nonsense, Hilda! You can't have changed. Haven't I been true to you? There's been no other girl. Unless—you haven't fallen for some other man, have you? One of those precious doctors of yours?"

"Certainly not! Why should I do that?"

"I don't know, I'm sure, but you're always going on about that wonderful Dr. Nairn. Wonderful he may be, but don't flatter yourself he would take up with a mere receptionist like you!"

It was the last straw. "Thank you very much! Let me tell you that Dr. Nairn thinks a lot more of me than you do. He's always kind and considerate. You say you care for me, Charles, but you only care for yourself."

"That will do, Hilda! I am bitterly disappointed in you."

"Then it's mutual."

They had reached the edge of town now, with few people around. Hilda took off her engagement ring and handed it to him. He marched straight on, unheeding.

"Put it back. I don't consider our engagement at an end. You've taken leave of your senses for a time, that's all, but you'll soon come back to them."

She replied quietly—"That's where you're wrong, Charles. If you don't take the ring back I—I'll throw it away. Over that wall," and she made a move to do so.

He caught her wrist. "Don't dare! That ring cost money!"

Money that he had grudged, she saw that now. She had always glossed over his tendency to meanness, but now she realized it would have ruined any chance of happiness. Better to go through life unmarried than be tied to a man with no generous instincts.

He pocketed the ring with the words, "You'll be sorry! Tomorrow you'll probably ask for it back. That's a woman all over."

"Not this woman," she told him finally. "I'm sorry Charles, but you're sure to meet someone else."

They had reached her gate. "I shan't ask you in. We'll say goodbye here." She held out her hand and he took it glumly.

"Well, if you're sure. But this has been a big blow to me."

A blow to his self-assurance if nothing else. He looked so crestfallen that she almost melted. But she had made her decision and must stick to it.

"Goodbye then," and she walked steadily away.

And so they parted, Hilda feeling a certain relief but still with a heavy heart. From now on, she and Charles would be mere nodding acquaintances. And the gossip that would ensue! His mother would be sure to put it round that he had been badly treated. She did not mind about that. There were many people who respected her too much to believe her heartless.

Yes, she had respect all right. But it was love she craved.

"There must be something wrong with me," she thought. "I'm not a lovable person and I might as well admit it. If I were only more like Cathy, outgoing and sweet." But what was the good of wishing.

CHAPTER EIGHT

THOUGH COLLEGE classes had been disbanded for the summer, Neil's research work at Loch Creenan still went on. He had finished the first draft of his textbook on marine zoology, but a lot remained to be done.

Each evening he retired to his study for the purpose of revision, but his eyes kept drifting across to the window opposite, discreetly curtained. No light in it; there was no need at this time of the year.

Besides, Cathy was not there. The sole reminder of their friendship was on the mantelpiece—a picture postcard of Kilgower. It showed a bay of yellow sand, jagged rock, and a blue sea, all against a background of majestic mountains.

There was writing on the card. "Here I am, home for a holiday—or longer, perhaps. It is every bit as beautiful as the picture. I am fitting in very well. There is a niche for me here and I am tempted to stay. Yours aye, Cathy." Just as brief as that.

The card had arrived two days ago, enclosed in an envelope. He had opened it eagerly, thinking she might have changed her mind about their parting. But no, the message said nothing except to convey the fact that he would possibly never see her again.

Closing his books, he went downstairs to the sitting room. His grandmother having gone to bed, his mother was alone. His heart contracted as he glimpsed her expression, unguarded for the moment. Evelyn Drummond had a soft, quiet beauty, once glowing, now resigned. As a boy he could recall flashes of high spirits, even incipient rebellion, but these had long since disappeared.

She raised her head. "How nice of you to come down and keep me company!"

"I ought to do it oftener," he told her. "You've been lonely since Dad went into the hospital. It's good to think he's getting home tomorrow."

"Yes, Neil, but I'm dreading it a little. Is that wicked of me?"

He smiled. "Not wicked—natural! He's not the easiest patient. And I'm the one who seems to upset him most. I sometimes wonder if I ought to find a place of my own."

She caught his sleeve pleadingly. "No, Neil, please! This house needs you. We all need you, especially myself."

"I know." He patted her hand reassuringly. "We need each other. And I could get on fine with Dad if he would only give in about Cathy. Do you think there's any chance?"

"I doubt it. For myself, I would welcome your Cathy. She has a sunny nature, would inject some vitality into this household! I am sure you love her, Neil, but your father is so set against her!"

"Don't I know it! And now I daren't even mention the subject. I'm fond of Dad, but his attitude is fast estranging us. To regard your own father as an enemy doesn't make for harmony, does it?"

It was the first time they had had a real talk about the dilemma he faced. He knew instinctively that she was on his side and that her loyalty to her husband was sorely tried. It wasn't only his problem; it was hers, too.

"Oh Neil, what would I give to see you both happy and reconciled!"

He took her hand in his. "Please don't distress yourself, Mom! It's not your fault. There's nothing you can do."

"That's what worries me most." Nothing she could do. It was a sad confession to make to the son she loved.

In the hour which followed these two came closer to each other than they had been since his childhood. He recalled little incidents they had laughed at together in happier times. Susan Brodie figured largely in their reminiscences. In those days she had shared their lives more. Grandmamma's presence was less intrusive, and his father was immersed in his once flourishing business.

When Neil went to fetch him from hospital next day, Andrew Drummond was up and dressed. The greeting was restrained, the journey back almost silent. Neil still had a painful memory of their last evening and so, no doubt, had his father.

The invalid seemed slightly improved in health, however, his movements only slightly slower, his speech still distinguishable. When the car drew up at Airlie House, Susan was there to help, and the stairs were safely negotiated.

"You're looking more like yourself," she commented. "They've been good to you in the hospital."

Andrew agreed. "Good to be home, though," he conceded, as his wife came forward to take his arm. "Thanks, Evelyn. I'm back again to bother you."

"No bother," and she led him to his old seat in the room.

Grandmamma was there too, managing affairs as usual. With three women in charge, Neil felt free to leave. Garaging the car, he took a stroll around the Square, whose gardens were full of roses in bloom. Pity Cathy was missing the roses, but there were roses in Kilgower and much, much more.

"There is a niche for me here." Of course there was, it was her home. Her friends were there and all her old associations. No wonder she was tempted to stay! But if she did, this weight would never lift from his heart.

Passing the Medical Center, which was closing for the lunch hour, he saw Hilda Baxter emerging and heading for the bus stop. He hesitated, uncertain whether to stop her. How much did she know about Cathy and himself?

But Hilda had seen him and had stopped of

her own volition. He went forward eagerly.

She smiled a greeting. "You wanted to know about Cathy?"

"That's right. Have you heard from her? I've just had a postcard."

"I had a letter this morning. She seems to be enjoying herself."

"So I gathered. Established herself in Kilgower again. Says she's tempted to stay. Did she mean it, do you think?"

"Well," replied Hilda, "there's nothing to keep her here, I suppose."

He flushed under her gaze. "Nothing, except— No doubt she told you about—us?"

She nodded—"Yes, and I'm sorry."

"Hilda, you know Cathy so well. Will she ever come back to Nethershaw? She has so many friends at home. Do you happen to know if there's anyone special?" The thought had been haunting him.

"She did mention there had been somebody before she came here, but I don't think it was serious. I wouldn't worry if I were you."

"Thank you. Cathy thinks a lot of you, Hilda. She says you may be getting married soon."

She shook her head. "That's all off. No happy ending for me. I hope you and Cathy have better fortune! Well, I'd better go for my bus. 'Bye for now."

She hurried off and Neil went on his way. From what he knew of Charles Ford, she was better off without him. Still, you could see the girl was unhappy. He was glad that Cathy, at least, was enjoying life. If her old affair were renewed, he couldn't blame her. Hadn't she often declared that waiting was a thing she could not do? He smiled ruefully, recalling Aunt Jessie's dictum: "Cathy can't wait. She just lunges at things."

Hilda joined the queue waiting at the bus stop. She was still feeling lost, like one jerked out of a rut onto an unknown road. Life stretched before her with no clue as to which way to turn, no sense of purpose.

The bus was a long time in coming. She was about to start walking, when a car stopped beside her and she recognized Dr. Nairn. Lately, the quiet but friendly doctor had become quite taciturn and she was surprised when he offered her a lift. She hung back.

"Thank you very much, but I'd be taking you out of your way."

"Not at all. I'm going to the hospital. That's in your direction, isn't it?"

She agreed and got inside. He drove on with a set face.

"This is kind of you, doctor."

"I wouldn't do it for everybody," he confessed. "Especially today."

She felt obliged to ask—"Why today?"

"I've a lot on my mind. Someone I love is there, in the hospital. He is not expected to live."

"Oh, I am sorry." He must be speaking of his young brother, the handicapped boy whom he had devoted himself to. "Could I possibly do something to help?"

"You are a great help as it is. So dependable in every way. That's why I can talk to you."

She felt a sense of uplift. "Please do. I think perhaps you keep things too much to yourself."

"So, you are giving the doctor advice? Not that I don't need it. My big problem is—should I hope for Robbie's recovery when I know it is better he should go? He's getting so much worse, Hilda. As it is, his life span has been longer than anyone hoped for."

"Because of you," she murmured. "Oh yes, I've heard how good you've been to him. Everybody at the Center admires and respects you."

No more was said until they turned into her road and stopped at the gate.

"I'm glad I met you, Hilda. Perhaps I'll even take your advice."

"I'll give you more any time you like," she told him with a smile. "Robbie and you will be in my thoughts, I assure you."

He replied huskily—"It's a comfort to know that. Please keep us in your thoughts!"

She looked after him, a constriction in her throat. Dr. Nairn needed her. To fill that need was enough purpose to keep her going on.

Evelyn Drummond had noticed a difference in her husband since his homecoming. He did not complain so much. Still morose, he seemed more grateful for what she did for him. Perhaps the hospital discipline had made him more appreciative of home comforts.

So ran her thoughts one evening as she sat with him in the room. Gran was upstairs and Neil was out. Relations were so strained between

Neil and his father that he often escaped. It was a state of affairs painful to everybody. Andrew sat there brooding, chin on chest, the picture of despondency. With all the brightness she could muster, Evelyn rallied him.

"Cheer up, Andrew! Would you like me to read to you?"

He lifted shadowed eyes to meet hers. "I'd rather you talk to me. We never talk."

It was true. Heart to heart confessions had long since ceased between them. His conversation had grown more dogmatic with the years, silencing any discussion. Evelyn was easily silenced. Faint protests were useless, and she had not the will for battle.

"What would you like to talk about?" she asked.

"Anything. No, that's not true. There's only one thing. Us."

"You and me, you mean?"

"Yes, and Neil, our son. Why won't he be friends with me?"

"You know why," she replied. "You have come between him and the woman he loves."

He looked puzzled. "Is he really in love with her?"

"I believe he is, and you have made him very unhappy." She waited for an outburst but none came. Instead of retaliating in the way she'd feared, he held out a shaky hand. She clasped it in hers.

"Oh, Andrew!" Tears rose in her eyes.

"Evelyn, my love."

Not for years had he called her that. A rush

of hope swept through her. She had told Neil there was nothing she could do but perhaps there was. It only needed courage. Andrew still loved her. Perhaps he would listen to her.

"Couldn't you forget your grudge against Jessie Paterson, Andrew? It's souring all our lives."

He withdrew his hand. "You're asking too much, Evelyn. That woman—"

" 'That woman' is just like the rest of us—human. She has a temper like yourself: she sticks up for her rights as she sees them. One can't undo what's happened in the past, but one can forget it."

It was a very long speech for her, the longest she had made for years without contradiction.

"I couldn't forget," he muttered.

"You could try. Promise me you'll try, Andrew!"

After a silence, he put out his hand again. His loose clasp seemed to gain strength from hers.

"All right, I'll do my best. Tell Neil he can bring the girl to see me."

"Oh, thank you!" Her eyes shone. "You've made me so happy!"

"You've been good to me, Evelyn, and you deserve to be happy."

With an arm round his shoulder, she laid her cheek against his.

"I love you, Andrew. Do you still love me?"

In a broken voice he replied. "With all my heart. In those lonely hours in the hospital, I longed for you."

They sat smiling at each other, until a footstep was heard at the door.

"It's your mother," she said, her smile fading.

Old Mrs. Drummond came into the room, her presence dominating it as usual.

"Not in bed yet, Andrew? You should not have let him stay up so late, Evelyn."

"It's all right, Gran, we were talking."

"As if you hadn't all day to talk! You look tired, Andrew. You know what the doctor said—plenty of rest."

There was nothing for Evelyn to do but make a move to the bedroom and get her husband settled for the night. His compliance touched her; it was so unlike the old Andrew. He caught her sleeve before she left him.

"My mother . . . She's been a thorn in your flesh all these years."

"Oh no! Just a wee bit aggravating at times."

"You're an angel to put up with her. You'll go on doing it, Evelyn?"

She nodded assent. "For your sake."

"But don't put up with too much. Speak out."

"I'm not much good at speaking out, but I'll do my best."

Then she left him to rejoin her mother-in-law who was fussily putting things to rights in the room.

"Susan will do that in the morning, Grandmamma."

She sniffed. "Susan's ideas of tidiness are not mine. Neil isn't in yet—? I wonder where he's gone."

"He didn't say and I didn't ask him. After

all, he's a man, not a boy. It's not for us to inquire."

"As long as he hasn't gone to that girl!"

With unwonted spirit the other replied—"If he has, it's perfectly all right. Andrew doesn't mind. He wants him to bring Cathy to the house."

In disbelief—"It's not true! He would never give in, just like that."

"Not just like that, Gran. He must have thought it over in the hospital. A bit of persuasion from me was all that was required."

"Huh. I'm sure he didn't mean it. He's not himself. Better not encourage Neil to bring the girl here. The sight of her would just bring on another bad turn."

"On the other hand, it might bring him and Neil together again. That's what I'm hoping."

"Hope what you like," was the response. "As for me, I do not wish to meet her. She is quite the wrong sort of girl for Neil. I intend to do my best to keep those two apart!"

Neil came home late. He had taken the car to the foot of Ben Creenan, then climbed steadily, leaving the world behind.

The scene that stretched around him had an unbelievable beauty. Pale in the evening light, the loch lay still and sleeping. Hills and valleys made a picture in varying shades of green. The blue of the sky merged into turquoise around the distant mountain tops.

He was quite alone up here to enjoy the beauty, but his craving was to share it with someone. He recalled what the poet had said—

"But grant me still a friend in my retreat, to whom to whisper—solitude is sweet." The presence of Cathy beside him was the only thing lacking in all this perfection. Without her, there would always be a lack. He returned home, despondent.

His mother opened the door to him. Her face was bright; he had not seen that sparkle in her eyes for a very long time.

"Sorry I'm late. Forgive your erring son?" he asked, kissing her.

"Nothing to forgive. I've something to tell you, Neil."

He followed her into the room. When they had settled down and his pipe was lit, she went on.

"Your Dad and I had a long talk tonight. He has changed, Neil, and that goes for me, too. I actually had the temerity to speak to him about Cathy."

Alarmed—"But, Mom, should you?"

"I ought to have done it before. I've been too remiss at speaking out my mind. It appears that Andrew has been having second thoughts."

"About Cathy, you mean?" he asked eagerly.

"Yes, indeed. He took it calmly, Neil. He even said you were to bring her here to see him."

He gazed at her, pipe in hand, only half believing.

"But that is wonderful! Are you sure?"

She nodded, smiling. "Quite sure. Of course, it's only a beginning, but that bitterness of his seems to be melting."

"Thank heaven for that!"

"So you'll bring her here, won't you, Neil?"

"Won't I, just!" Then, more soberly, "There's only one hitch. She's not here; she's gone home. Not for good, I hope. I'll go and fetch her back tomorrow. I've nothing on hand that can't be put off."

"But there's no need for such haste, surely."

"Very much need. There's not a minute to lose. I must make sure of her before it's too late."

"It's not like you to be in such a hurry."

"I guess not," he laughed, "but I'm in love. I'm going to bring back that girl and marry her immediately!"

"Oh dear," she sighed. "You'll have to have patience, Neil. You'll do nothing to upset Dad?"

"I promise." He was on his feet and would have started the journey that night had it been possible.

"At least you'll let Cathy know you're on the way?"

"No, I want to surprise her. To see her face when I appear. First thing tomorrow, I'll have a word with her aunt to get instructions. Yes, and then—" his mind ran on as he made for the door. Then, impulsively, he came back to catch his mother in his arms.

"You're the best mother that ever was and I love you!"

How sweetly these words sounded to her, he would never know.

Jessie Paterson was due for a surprise next morning as she sorted out the bundles of newspapers that had just arrived. It was too early for customers, and she was alone when Neil strode into the shop.

"Good morning, Aunt Jessie!"

She eyed him reprovingly. "I'm not your aunt, nor likely to be."

"Don't be too sure. I'm going to see Cathy today to ask her a question. Can you guess what it is?"

Her nose gave its customary twitch. "She'll not marry you, if that's what you mean. As long as your father— "

"My father," he told her, "has asked to see Cathy. He might even ask to see you one of these days."

"Huh," she sniffed, "he can ask on his bended knees. I vowed never to go over the door of Airlie House and I'm not shifting now."

"All right," he laughed, "we'll cross that bridge when we come to it. What I came for was to ask how to get to Kilgower and where to find Cathy there. There was no address on my postcard."

"You're going to Kilgower! But it's hundreds of miles— "

"I have a perfectly good car. Come on, Aunt Jessie, tell me!"

With a show of reluctance but secretly thrilled, she complied. He could not fail to find the route, which ran through Glencoe and Fort William.

"Kilgower's just a village beside the sea, not on the map."

"That's all right. There are signposts and

I've a tongue in my head."

"You'll need it if you're going to persuade her. She seems perfectly happy to be home. She's made it up with her stepmother and everything in the garden's lovely." Then, regretfully—"I'm going to miss her if she stays."

"Don't worry, I'll do all in my power to bring her back."

"Then, good luck to you." He shook the hand she proferred and went out to his car.

Cathy Paton knocked at the door of her father's office and peeped in. The last patient of the afternoon had just left and he was still at his desk.

"Marjory says tea's ready, Dad. Will you come for it?"

He sat back, regarding her with a smile. "Sure, in a minute. You're looking well, Cath. Kilgower agrees with you."

"Yes, Dad, I feel the better for my holiday."

"But surely it's more than a holiday? Now that you and Marjory are on good terms, you'll surely stay. Everybody is glad you're back. Especially your old friend, Jim Mackenzie. I heard about you and him at the dance last night!"

She blushed. "Whatever you heard isn't true. We just danced that's all."

"All night, I gather. But why not? Jim's a man after my own heart. You'd do well to take him."

"Nonsense, Dad. He hasn't asked me."

"But he will. You like him, don't you?"

"Of course I like him." Jim, her old love, had a charm which had once nearly swept her off her feet. She had resisted it, feeling that he didn't come up to her ideal, but it would have been easy to give in. It still would be easy if she had never met Neil Drummond.

Leaving her father, she went through the passageway that connected her father's office with the house, where her stepmother was waiting with the tea things.

"Dad's just coming, Marjorie."

The woman who had been the cause of her leaving home, asked—

"Will you have a cup while we're waiting?"

"No, thanks. I'll go for a walk, I think."

These two had come to understand each other a little better. With both making an effort, relations between them were now quite cordial. Cathy had realized that her father needed a person like Marjorie to look after him. She was conscientious and a good manager. Secure in the knowledge of her husband's love, she now felt she had no cause for jealousy.

She went on, frankly—"You love Kilgower, don't you, Cathy?"

"Yes, I do. There's no place like it."

"Then," she said sincerely, "please stay on. Your father wishes it and I'd like it myself, truly."

It was a generous gesture. Cathy gave her a warm smile.

"Thanks, Marjorie, it's kind of you. The

truth is, I'm still trying to make up my mind. It's about time I decided. I'll think about it while I'm out, I promise."

Leaving the house, which was on the sea front, she took her favorite stroll along the shore. There, perched on a high rock surrounded by all the sights and sounds she loved, she felt she might never have been away. To remain here and forget all that had happened might not be so difficult. The might-have-been would slip out of her memory in time. Or would it? With the thought, a terrible yearning came over her, and she knew that, however long the years, she would never forget.

Absorbed in her thoughts, she was only half aware of a figure coming toward her across the turf which divided her from the road. Not one of the villagers, probably a summer visitor. Still, he might have known better than to intrude on her privacy; weren't there miles of shore all empty to right and left?

She looked again and her heart gave a great leap. But of course she was dreaming. Neil Drummond was hundreds of miles away—it was not possible.

There he was, however, the man she loved. She slid off her rock, leaning on it for support. The glad surprise on her face more than fulfilled Neil's expectations.

"Are you real?" she gasped.

"Try me," he said and caught her up in his arms. "There!" and he kissed her full on the lips. "Is that real enough for you?"

"Neil, we'll be seen!"

"Only by the seagulls."

"But why are you here?"

He replied masterfully—"To take you back where you belong."

"But this is my place," she demurred.

"Your place, Cathy, is with me. My father has asked to see you. You'll come home with me?"

It took her a moment or two to get her breath back. Then, with no hesitation, she replied—

"Yes, of course. When?"

"Tomorrow, first thing. I was on my way to your house when I saw you on that rock."

"You must have eagle's eyes," she told him.

"Yes, where you are concerned."

In the car, he told her what had taken place in Airlie House.

"But what if your father doesn't take to me after all?" she asked.

"He will. How could he help it?"

"And your mother?"

"She's already in favor. So is Aunt Jessie; she wished me luck. Everybody's in favor. We can get married any time."

The prospect seemed too dazzling to be true.

"Wait a minute," she said. "Did you say—everybody? What about your grandmother?"

He hesitated. "Oh, Gran, will just have to toe the line."

With those words, came Cathy's first doubt. She could not see old Mrs. Drummond meekly "toeing the line."

"She won't, Neil. She'll make trouble."

"Nonsense! Don't let that thought enter your head."

But the thought, once there, refused to go away.

CHAPTER NINE

JESSIE PATERSON WAS closing her shop when Neil's car drew up in the vacant parking space. She stood waiting. He came out to open the door for Cathy, who stepped on to the pavement, dazzling her aunt with a smile.

So, the young man had managed to persuade her to return. We're in for it now, thought Jessie. The pair looked as if nothing would move them from the course they had chosen.

"I told you I'd bring her back," announced Neil.

"Oh well, what's to be is to be."

"Exactly," laughed Cathy. "Is there anything to eat upstairs?"

"I thought your minds would be above food," remarked Jessie, leading the way, "but I put a steak pie in the oven just in case."

In spite of being so much in love, the pair did justice to the meal. They were on top of the world. In fact, thought Jessie, they were in another world altogether. "Let them bide there as long as they can. They'll soon be brought down to earth!"

"You seem to be taking things for granted," she ventured, as she and Cathy washed up, Neil having taken his leave.

"Not quite. There will be a few hurdles yet, Auntie. But nothing can stop us now!"

"Not even if I refuse to be on speaking terms with the Drummonds?"

Cathy took her arm pleadingly: "You wouldn't do that to us?"

Jessie sniffed. "I don't know. I once vowed never to enter that house. They'll have to unbend a lot to make me break that vow!"

"They will, I'll see to it! All the same, I'm rather dreading tomorrow, when Neil takes me to see his Dad. I'll feel like an exhibit, to be inspected and perhaps rejected. I've no airs or graces, Auntie, and I can't be anything but myself."

"And don't try," she was advised, "for it wouldn't work. If all goes well, when will the wedding be?"

Cathy said hopefully, "In the autumn."

Jessie shook her head. "Too soon. Marriage isn't a thing to lunge at!"

"I'd rather 'lunge' than wait four years, like Hilda."

"And your father—what does he think of all this?" demanded her Aunt.

"He likes Neil. I took him along to the house, and they sat up last night talking. I'm sure he'll be pleased to have him for a son-in-law. Any father would!"

Yes, she had no qualms about her father. Qualms she did have, however, about tomorrow's ordeal. As she went to her room to prepare for bed, she felt her confidence ebbing. There would be no sleep for her tonight.

Looking out of her window in the gray light, she could see the cold rectangle of Neil's window across the yard. As she gazed longingly, a light was switched on, sending cheer into the night.

Then Neil himself appeared, gazing across. He was waving to her and blowing kisses. Laughing, she sent him back kisses galore. She felt better now. Confidence was surging back again.

Neil called for Cathy next afternoon. In a simple summer frock, with her fair hair flowing free and her candid blue eyes smiling into his, she had a charm which no one could resist. His father would be less than human if he did not take her to his heart. So, hopefully, ran Neil's thoughts as they climbed the steps to Airlie House. Halfway, she hesitated. "I'd feel much better going in by the back door!"

Taking her arm firmly—"You're not kitchen company today. Come on, there's nothing to be afraid of!"

Susan Brodie opened the door with a flourish. As usual, she was up-to-date on the romance and was proud of it. Hadn't she suspected it from the first?

"They're in the sitting room, all of them," and, leading the way, she opened the door.

"Hello, folks," Neil began, "here's Cathy to see you."

Cathy stepped inside, her eyes taking in the three people who had turned to gaze at her. It was an awesome moment. True, Evelyn Drummond was smiling as she rose to greet her; but her husband remained crouched in his seat, his look non-committal. The old lady on the other hand was regarding her with stern disapproval. Then, face tight, she suddenly got to her feet, her hand on her stick, and marched to the door.

"Gran, won't you stay?" Neil's hand went out to stop her, but she brushed it off and left the room without a word. Evelyn broke the silence—

"Never mind Gran, Cathy! If she is not pleased to see you, I am and so is Neil's father. Aren't you, Andrew?"

The dim eyes were still studying her. Cathy hung back till she saw a shaky hand being held out. She went forward to clasp it, and remained there, her hand in his.

"I hope you're feeling better, Mr. Drummond?" Her voice shook a little.

Without replying to her question, he said, "Come nearer . . . my sight—"

She bent toward him, smiling.

"You're bonnie," he faltered. "Bonnie," and that was all.

"Come sit here, Cathy." Neil pulled forward a chair.

For about a minute no one seemed to know what to say. Then Evelyn asked,

"Did you enjoy your holiday in Kilgower?"

Cathy's eyes lit up. "Oh yes! It's my home, you know."

"Tell us about it."

Forgetting her shyness, she waxed eloquent about her Highland home, her father's work there, the scenic beauty, and the people. She even told them about the dances and the songfests.

"Cathy shines at the songfests," said Neil proudly. "She's a singer, you know."

"I've heard her in the choir," observed his mother.

Mr. Drummond moved in his chair. "What kind of songs do you sing?"

"Mostly Hebridean," she told him.

Neil had an idea: "Sing us one now. Please, Cathy!" He moved to the piano. He knew her favorites and began to play "Mairi's Wedding."

Tossing back her hair, she took a deep breath and began. "Step we gaily as we go; Heel for heel and toe for toe."

She sang infectiously, so that the joyful lilt of the music filled the room. Feet began tapping, and Mr. Drummond's frail fingers followed the beat on the arm of his chair.

"Good tune that," he observed. "What about another?"

She sang many songs both sad and glad until Susan brought in afternoon tea. She felt more at home now, as if she were beginning to belong.

Grandma Drummond did not come down for tea, however. It was the only small hitch in the proceedings. Neil took her home, well pleased.

"You've captured their hearts, just as you did mine," he told her on the way upstairs.

"I wouldn't know about that," she said doubtfully, "but as long as I didn't put them off me—your father was very nice, not the stern parent I expected. I think I could get on with him."

"Show me the person you couldn't get on with!"

"Well, take your grandmother, for one."

"Even my Gran won't be able to hold out very long."

"Don't be too sure about that! She's very determined to keep me out of the family." She caught his arm. "You won't let her, will you Neil?"

"No, darling, I shan't let her. Don't you know the strength of my love for you?"

Reaching the top of the stairs, he took her in his arms, and Jessie was just in time to witness a long, rapturous kiss.

"I must say you might have waited till you got inside," she remarked. "There must be something about my doormat—it had that effect on you once before."

Neil laughed. "She's right, Cathy. But we hardly knew each other then."

"And you think you know each other now?" said Jessie dryly. "You've hardly started yet."

Two days later, Cathy was back at the Medical Center. She arrived early, hoping to have a word with Hilda before the day's work began.

Her friend was in the cloakroom, regarding herself critically in the mirror.

"Top of the morning, Hilda!"

She jumped round, face brightening. "Cathy! Oh, thank goodness. I was afraid you might not come back."

"I was brought back, willy nilly, by you know who," was the reply.

"Neil Drummond? Oh, I'm glad. It's all right, then, you'll be getting engaged?"

"Probably married, too, before very long. Will you be my bridesmaid, Hilda?"

"Willingly. I know all about being a bridesmaid. This will be my third time. Three times a bridesmaid, never a bride," she finished sadly.

"But that's nonsense. What about Charles?"

Hilda shook her head, her fine gray eyes clouding over. "Charles belongs to the past. We quarrelled."

"But you'll make it up?"

"Never . . . I don't love him any more. Cathy. I was too cowardly to own up before; I did so want a home—a family! But I wouldn't have been happy. I know that now."

Cathy took her hand. "It must have been hard, but I'm sure you were right. He wasn't good enough for you! Someone else will come along, never fear."

Hilda laughed ruefully. "Too late for that. No, Cathy, I'm fated for the single life. I've got nieces and nephews; I'll work hard at being an auntie."

No doubt Hilda would make a splendid aunt, but she was more than suited for wifehood and motherhood.

"It's not fair! You'd be such a super partner. Especially with your medical knowledge. A doctor, now. Why not Doctor Nairn?" She spoke half jokingly and was surprised to see Hilda's flushed face. "You like him?"

"Yes, I do—" she said defiantly, but I'm far from the poor man's thoughts at the moment. You knew about his brother being ill? Well, he died, Cathy; the funeral was the other day. He had devoted his life to him, and now he's down in the depths."

"So that's why you look so sad. I feel quite guilty at being so happy myself. I don't really deserve it."

"If anybody deserves it, you do," declared Hilda. She was genuinely glad that Cathy had achieved the "happy ending" she had so longed for herself.

Not for the first time, Hilda wished that she had something of Cathy's outgoing nature. Withdrawn and self-critical, she found it difficult to make friends. Recently she had imagined that Dr. Nairn was taking more notice of her, but since his brother's death he had remained aloof. There was a barrier between them that she could not break down. She was still thinking about him when, her shift over, she made her way to the bus stop. No one noticed her among the crowd. Her calm face, quiet gray eyes, and thoughtful expression did not immediately attract attention; it was only on closer acquaintance that one realized the depths that were hidden there.

Hilda had no sooner joined the bus queue than she was aware that, once again, Dr. Nairn had drawn up in hopes of giving her a lift.

"Going home?" he asked curtly.

"Yes, but please don't bother—"

He opened the car door. "No bother. Come

on, get in." She did so, and he gave his attention to the traffic while she studied his face, so tired, so gray that she longed to give him comfort. Almost without thinking, she said aloud:

"You're very tense, Doctor. I'm worried about you."

He flicked her a look—"You? worried about me?"

"Yes, I am. I don't believe you're taking care of yourself."

"Of course I am!" he denied crossly. "You know nothing about me."

"I know you have suffered a loss and you are blaming yourself in some way. Yet everybody knows how you devoted yourself to that boy. No one could have done more."

"Thank you. Have you ever lost somebody you cared for very much?" His tone was bitter.

"Not in that way, but no doubt I shall some day."

"There's only one way to prevent it," he went on. "Don't let yourself get too attached to anyone. It only leads to heartache and regret."

"I know," reflected Hilda. "But isn't it all worth it, in some strange way?"

He gave a short laugh. "You may think so, but I don't. From now on, I shall guard my feelings, be my own master."

She was silent. There seemed nothing more to say. She had done her best, but the tenuous tie between them seemed to have broken.

He stopped at her gate. "Sorry, Hilda; I'm not very bright company, but you won't have to put up with me for much longer."

"What do you mean?" she asked fearfully.

"I'll be leaving Nethershaw soon to fill a vacancy up north. Fresh fields and pastures new, you know."

Her heart contracted. "Oh, no!"

"Oh, yes. It's the only way to forget. Keep it to yourself, will you?"

"Yes, but you're going to be missed. I'll miss you," she said frankly.

"Thanks, but you have plenty to fill your young life. 'Bye now, and thanks for trying to cheer me up. I promise I shall take care of myself. Will that please you?"

A smile flickered momentarily as he waved her off. Numbed, Hilda watched the car move away. Only now did she realize how much her work at the Center had depended on the friendship and encouragement of this man ... without him, she did not see how she could carry on.

A well-known jeweler had recently opened a shop in Nethershaw, and it was here that Neil took Cathy one sunny August day to buy an engagement ring.

Standing arm in arm at the shop window, studying the rings, they were oblivious of the passersby. Some went past with a smile; it was only too obvious what these two were after! But on Celia Carr's face, there was no smile, merely a look of chagrin and disbelief. She had heard rumors, but this seemed a certainty.

"Nice day," she remarked airily. "Long time no see!"

Neil turned; he had almost forgotten there was such a person.

"Yes, it's a long time," he agreed. "You have met Cathy before, haven't you, Celia?"

"Once or twice. In her aunt's shop and at the Medical Center. Last time, she was on crutches."

Cathy remembered the day well. Celia had more than hinted that she and Neil were back on the old footing.

"Have you got over your broken ankle, or whatever it was?" she inquired.

"Long ago." Cathy was still holding Neil's arm. He put his hand on top of hers:

"Congratulate us, Celia!"

With true acting ability, Celia produced a dazzling smile.

"Certainly. Actually, I did guess that something was in the wind. Congratulations, both; I hope you'll be very happy!" And she shook hands with them both, showing not the slightest discomfiture.

When she had gone on, Cathy remarked, "It's good of her to wish us happiness. She must be feeling terrible."

"Why must she?"

"She was in love with you, Neil."

"Probably thought she was. Somebody much better will turn up for Celia, don't worry."

"There couldn't possibly be anybody better," she protested.

He squeezed her arm. "Which only shows

from his parents, who needed him so much, yet they would be independent of them.

"It sounds quite thrilling," she concurred. "Of course I'll have a look!"

It was Susan who let them in by the back door. The kitchen premises were on the left as they entered, the garden flat on the right. But first, Cathy had to show off her ring.

"Look, Susan, you're the first one to see it."

"My, oh, my," exclaimed the warmhearted housekeeper. "Not that I didn't guess! You're a real nice lass and I wish you joy!" With that she took Cathy into a warm embrace.

"Hey, don't you poach on my preserves," objected Neil. "We're going to inspect the flat, Susan, but mum's the word."

They went along a corridor, to be greeted by a burst of sunshine pouring through the large, low window of the living room. Outside, a tangle of flowers and bushes was enclosed by a mossy stone wall.

"The garden's private; we'd have it to ourselves."

There was a summer house, too, overgrown by creepers. Inside were two smaller rooms and a kitchen with an old-fashioned sink and rusty stove.

"You'd have everything new here, of course, just like the modern kitchens in the advertisements," he promised. "Same in the bathroom. As for wallpaper and all that, you'd have fun choosing it, wouldn't you?"

Her eyes were dancing. "I could make this into a dream house! Oh Neil, when can we begin?"

"Just now if you like. Come and tell Dad what you think of it."

She followed him through to the sitting room. No longer was she doubtful of her reception there. Neil's parents were already more than reconciled to the prospect of accepting her as a daughter, in Evelyn's case, the daughter she had always yearned for. The ring was admired, and the subject of the garden flat was discussed.

Evelyn drew Cathy aside. "Neil and his Dad are keen on this, Cathy, and so am I, of course. But I don't want you to feel you've got to agree."

"It's not like that at all," she assured her. "I love that flat already, and think what we could do to it!"

"But living so near us. Some girls might object— "

"Not this girl. I think I'm very lucky. May I kiss you?"

Evelyn's laugh was becoming more frequent these days. The young life that the house so much needed was beginning to make a difference already. Her husband was much more amenable, and she looked forward to the time when, if providence was kind, there would be grandchildren to lighten their days.

"The garden will need a lot of attention," she was saying when the door suddenly opened and Grandmamma Drummond, a tall figure in black, stood there frowning at them. She had withdrawn more and more to her own room of late, and they were surprised to see her. Neil at once jumped up and offered her a chair.

"Come sit down, Gran. You're just in time to hear our plans."

She did not move. "What plans?"

"Just this. Cathy and I are going to take over the garden flat. Isn't that grand?"

The newcomer stood stiffly, still frowning.

"The garden flat is not fit for human habitation."

"But it's going to be! Would you like to hear about the alterations we've planned? Come on, here's a chair—" and he went forward to take her arm. She stepped back, pushing him aside.

"I don't wish to hear about your plans, thank you. They have nothing to do with me, except this. If you marry this girl and come here to live, I shall leave Airlie House."

Her son jerked up his head—"You can't do that, Mamma!"

"I can and I will. If these two come in, I go out, and that's that!"

With that, she turned her back and left the room, closing the door behind her with a bang.

Neil asked—"Shall I go after her?"

"No," said his father. "Let her be. She'll come to her senses. She knows Airlie House is her home—where else would she go?"

"You're right, there's nowhere."

Cathy put in, shakily. "If it means trouble, Neil, we'd better forget about the garden flat."

"Not at all," maintained Mr. Drummond. "My mother likes her own way. This time she's not going to get it. You and Neil go ahead and I'll uphold you."

"There's something else," Evelyn told them,

with a glance at her husband. "We would like your aunt to come to tea with us, if she cares. Will you ask her, Cathy?"

Cathy said she'd be glad to. The sore question of Aunt Jessie had not been touched upon. Neil had said "Bide your time; the reconciliation will come."

Now it seemed to be imminent. It all depended on Aunt Jessie herself.

Cathy couldn't get up the stairs fast enough. When her aunt came to the door, she hugged her tightly.

"Oh, Auntie, we've got the ring and we're going to live in Airlie House and they want you to come to tea!"

"Hold on, one thing at a time." Jessie unclasped her arms and had a look.

"Ay, it's a bonnie ring. Take care of it. But this about you living in Airlie House—I'm not too sure."

Cathy explained that they would actually be on their own. "We'll visit often. You can help us to choose furniture and things. And you will come to tea, won't you, Auntie?"

Jessie parked herself on the sofa, the better to think.

"What if I said no?"

"You won't! It would ruin our happiness."

"Damn! I made a vow, you know."

"You can break it! If Neil's father can relent, surely you can too!"

Jessie rubbed her nose thoughtfully.

"There's no one else I would do it for, mind, but all right, Cathy."

Another hug, even tighter than the first, robbed her of breath.

And so, a few days later, Jessie went to tea in Airlie House. She was dressed in a very respectable navy dress and jacket, with a pink silk scarf at the neck. Cathy had done her aunt's hair the night before, and though the ends were a bit frizzy, it was orderly enough. Her cheeks were flushed, her nose more so, as they mounted the steps.

"I feel like Mary, Queen of Scots, going to her execution," she observed.

Cathy laughed. "It won't be as bad as that." And then Susan opened the door.

"At last," she said. "I'm right glad to see you, Jessie."

"Well, let me in and get it over!"

They were shown into the sitting room, and Evelyn rose to greet them.

"Welcome to Airlie House, Miss Paterson."

"Thank you, Mrs. Drummond." She then turned to Andrew, "And thank you, too."

Mr. Drummond cleared his throat—"A pleasure. Do be seated, please!"

Jessie sat down, very straight. With courage she went on—

"I'm glad our families are to be joined."

Andrew replied huskily. "I feel the same. We can forget the past, I think."

"Agreed," said Jessie, straight to the point as usual.

With that, they began to talk about other things. Jessie gave them tidbits of news about Nethershaw and the things that happened in the shop, all laced with her particular brand of humor, until she had them laughing heartily. Andrew's laugh was a bit rusty for lack of use, but that would come right in time, Cathy was sure.

Later, with tea, Neil came to join them, but again old Mrs. Drummond did not appear.

"How did I do?" asked Jessie when they got home.

"Splendidly, Auntie. I'm proud of you. That's the second last hurdle over and done with."

"The last being old Lady Drummond, I suppose? She's a hard nut to crack. You'll never do it, Cathy."

"She'll come round. Neil thinks so and so do his parents. Anyhow, she can't do anything very drastic!"

Any doubts disappeared in the excitement of getting the house ready. With the date fixed for the middle of October, there was little enough time, but the builders and decorators set to with a will. Cathy was kept busy at work, too, and with Neil being on extra duty at Loch Creenan, they did not see a great deal of each other. But it would be all right on the Day, and for ever and ever after.

Meanwhile the few hours spent together were touched with magic. One night they stood at the window of their future home looking out to the garden, on which a full moon shed a golden light, changing each plant and flower into something rich and strange.

"Just like people when they fall in love. Their whole life changes," said Cathy. Then she heaved a sigh.

"What's that for? I thought you were happy." Neil made her look at him. "Come on, tell me what's wrong?"

"Nothing, really. It's just—well, your grand-mother. She hasn't said one word to me; just glared as if she hated me. Couldn't we be extra nice to her, Neil? Give her a present or some-thing?"

He laughed. "As a reward for giving you hate looks? Strange reasoning."

"Well, we're supposed to do good to them that hate us. What would your Gran like for a present? You must know."

Neil pondered. "The only thing I can think of will make you laugh. She did say, some time ago, that she would like to possess one of these super deluxe Scrabble boards. But as she doesn't play Scrabble any more—"

"She might if you present her with a deluxe set. It's worth trying. Please, Neil!"

He could not deny her. "If you think it will do any good, I'll get one tomorrow."

He was as good as his word. When Cathy came the next night, the Scrabble game was there, done up in an enticing parcel.

"Let's go up and surprise her." Neil led the way upstairs. Cathy let him go in first before daring to show her face.

"Hello, Gran! Like a game of Scrabble?"

Then he stopped short, looking around in bewilderment. The room, overcrowded with his grandmother's old-fashioned furniture, looked as usual, but the straight-backed chair was empty.

"She isn't here, Cathy. She's gone off without a word!"

"But she can't have gone. She'll be downstairs, Neil."

"She is not! Look, Cathy, a note on the mantelpiece."

Taking it down, he hurriedly glanced over it.

"It's true. Gran has carried out her threat. Read that!"

CHAPTER TEN

CATHY TOOK THE NOTE from Neil. It was written in a large, angular hand, the hand of a woman who knew her own mind.

"When you get this, I shall have gone to stay in the Greenview Rest Home. Please do not try to contact me. And do not expect me to come to the wedding. I shall send for my things in due course. Esther Drummond."

"Well," breathed Cathy. "How do you think she got away without anyone knowing?"

"She has her own guile," observed Neil, "and the taxi office is just across the road. Trust Gran to upset our applecart. She deserves a good old-fashioned spanking."

"All very well, but this means the breakup of the Drummonds. Oh, Neil!"

He smoothed her hair, looking straight into her distressed eyes.

"It may be the breakup of the Drummonds, but it's not the breakup of you and me! If she hoped for that, she made a big mistake."

"But Neil, that Greenview place won't suit her at all. She'll be miserable there."

"Serve her right," he declared.

"Don't say that. I've passed that house, a big unfriendly place. There's a window looking out to the street. They sit there hour after hour—nothing to do, getting older and older. She can't stay there; we'll have to fetch her back!"

Neil disagreed. "You see what she says—don't try to contact her. You're much too soft-hearted, darling."

"Your father, Neil—how is he going to take this?"

"We'll see. Let's go and tell him."

Solemnly, they entered the sitting room. Evelyn was reading aloud to her husband. His expression as he looked at her was of love and tenderness. Smiling at the pair, he asked,

"Well, did Gran like her present?"

"She didn't get it," said Neil, handing him the note. Having read it, Andrew passed it to his wife.

"It has happened after all." But he showed no signs of shock, just sadness.

Evelyn's reaction was the same as Cathy's. "We'll have to get her back!"

Her husband pondered. "The more we press her, the firmer she will make her stand. Perhaps we should leave her alone."

But she who had most reason to resent the old lady's interference in the household shook her head.

"We can only try. What do you say, Neil?"

"Cathy thinks the same as you do, Mom. Soft-hearted, both of you. But if you like, I'll phone Greenview right away."

He dialed the number and asked for his grandmother. There was a long wait before the matron returned to tell him that Mrs. Drummond had retired for the night. "She says she does not wish to come to the phone."

"I'll come and see her tomorrow then."

"Sorry, but she has given strict instructions. No visitors."

Neil went back to the room and told them.

"That clinches it," declared his father. "Leave her alone. If she cares to come back, she may, but we shan't try to persuade her!"

Cathy went back home, feeling it was all her fault.

Aunt Jessie tried to comfort her. "Don't fret yourself, hen. Airlie House will be a better place without her and her domineering ways."

"But it's her home. There will be talk. They'll say that I displaced her. How can Neil and I be happy under these circumstances?"

"I don't suppose you will be, being you. But try to forget her, Cathy. You have plenty to think about getting ready for your wedding day."

True enough, every minute was occupied. Cathy was staying on her job after she was married to help with finances. Besides the preparations for the wedding, there were the renovations to the garden flat to inspect and admire, a highly exciting business.

Because of Mr. Drummond's health, the wedding was to be a quiet affair in the church in the Square, the guest list confined to members of both families and a few close friends. Aunt Jessie looked after ordering the wedding cake and the reception at a local hotel; she also saw to the wedding invitations, church flowers, and photographer and was in her element doing so.

If only old Mrs. Drummond had not thrown a wrench in the works everyone would have been happy. Her behavior threatened to spoil what would otherwise have been a wholly joyful occasion. In addition, Mr. Drummond's health was giving slight cause for anxiety, and Dr. Nairn started calling again. On his last visit before leaving for his new post, it fell to Cathy to show him out.

"Has Mr. Drummond been worrying about anything?" he asked, lingering on the step.

She told him the facts. "You must have heard that his mother is now living in Greenview. People are talking."

"I never listen to talk, you know."

"Yes, and you must miss a lot," she ventured.

"Really? One thing I did hear—that you are to be married soon."

"That's right. Hilda Baxter is to be my bridesmaid."

"Well! She never told me. When is her own wedding coming off?"

Cathy stared at him. "Wedding—Hilda? You are behind the times, Dr. Nairn. Hilda's engagement was broken off some time ago."

The man's face was a study. "She didn't tell me that either."

"I suppose she thought it wasn't medical business. Hilda is so conscientious. But surely you must have noticed she wasn't wearing her engagement ring?"

"And how would you expect a busy doctor to notice a thing like that?" he demanded.

"Not if it didn't concern him, I suppose."

From his stance on the middle step, he threw back the words—"But it does concern me. You women don't know everything!"

With which he disappeared into his car, starting off jerkily, quite unlike his usual self.

Cathy stood, quietly smiling. Was it possible? Was Hilda after all to gain her heart's desire?

Meanwhile, Hilda was living from day to day, dreading the approaching departure of the doctor she had served with such dedication. Though she had every intention of sticking to her job, for it was not in her nature to do otherwise, it was going to lack the necessary impetus—that of doing something for someone she cared about. The other doctors, though pleasant, were impersonal, whereas Dr. Nairn had always treated her with special consideration.

Hilda's mind these days was inclined to wander, and for the first time she was guilty of making errors; nothing serious, but the fact that she could do such a thing distressed her.

"Dr. Nairn wishes to see you," she was told at the end of her day. "You're in for it, Hilda!"

Her cheeks flamed. What awful mistake had she made now? She had at least hoped for a friendly farewell.

Expecting the worst, she knocked at his door and at a curt command went in. He was seated at his desk writing and did not look up.

"Sit down, please."

She took the chair opposite him, waiting, as if she were a patient.

"Yes, Miss Baxter?"

"You sent for me," she reminded him.

"So I did. He pushed aside his papers and his blue-gray eyes met hers directly. She shrank from that gaze.

"I am very annoyed with you, Miss Baxter."

She looked down, murmuring—"I'm sorry if I made a mistake. I—I haven't been quite myself lately. What have I done?"

He sat back, still eyeing her. "You have withheld from me a very vital piece of information."

She paled. "To do with a patient?"

"To do with yourself. Why did you not tell me you had broken off your engagement?"

Taken aback, she could only stammer—"I—well, I didn't think it would interest you."

"Interest me!" He got to his feet and strode restlessly to the window before confronting her. "Anything to do with you interests me. Did you not know that?"

"I thought you were interested only in the work I do for you, not because of anything personal. You are a very reserved person, Dr. Nairn. I thought, as a receptionist, you would like me to be the same. That was why I did not mention my broken engagement. I think—"

He stopped her. "You think too much, Hilda!" Then, gripping her by the arms he gave her a little shake. "You're not a bit like other girls. You might have given me some encouragement!"

She gave him a faint smile. "I simply don't know how."

"Then start now and try. That is, if you really wish to."

With a gulp—"Oh yes, I wish to, if you do."

"Of course I do! For a start—" a roguish twinkle danced in his eyes, "you can let me kiss you, right now."

She drew back, alarmed. "Dr. Nairn, that is not professional conduct!"

"Who cares?" Next minute, she was in his arms. He held her yearningly. "Oh Hilda, Hilda, I need you so much!"

She could not believe it was happening "I didn't know. You told me you would never allow yourself to get fond of anyone again."

"I said that in a moment of bitterness and I was wrong. Besides, one can't guard one's feelings to that extent. I tried hard not to fall in love with you, Hilda. You were engaged and not for me, I thought. Tell me, is it possible that you love me, just a little bit?"

She blinked away happy tears. "Not just a little bit. I love you very, very much, Doctor."

"David, please. And you'll come with me, Hilda, to the wilds up north?"

"Anywhere with you, David."

There followed more unprofessional conduct before Hilda emerged from the room, her cheeks burning.

"Well, did he put you through the mill?" the others asked her.

They had never heard the solemn Hilda laugh so lightheartedly.

"I suppose you might call it that," she said.

that love is blind; but please go on thinking that!"

They went into the shop. Cathy told herself this was the most thrilling moment of her life, but there were so many thrilling moments these days it was difficult to decide. The ring she chose was a plain band with a solitaire diamond.

"Are you sure you want that one? I might stretch to something a bit more showy."

"I don't like 'showy' things, and I never, never want you to stretch your resources to please me," she declared. "I know you can't be very rich, but I'm good at managing, Neil. I managed for my father, you know."

"You can manage *for* me as long as you don't try to manage *me*," he laughed. "My Gran tries that and doesn't succeed."

The ring had the added charm of fitting perfectly.

"And now to fix the date," he said on the way home.

"Also, where we're going to live. I've got an idea; but if you don't like it, say so."

She was agog to hear.

"The garden flat of Airlie House hasn't been used for a long time. Dad and I were talking about it last night. He could get workmen on the job immediately. It's completely separate, with an entrance at the back. You could see it now before making up your mind."

Their previous discussions about a house had been vague and inconclusive. This was something definite. Neil would not be separated

Cathy had a week's leave before her wedding. On her way to inquire about the progress of the wedding cake from the baker's, she ran into Hilda.

"Hello, there. It's time we had à talk about things. I'm going into Mackay's. Have you time for a coffee?"

"Plenty. I've done my stint for the day." And they linked arms as they walked.

Shortly, they were smiling at each other across a table for two.

"You look different," mused Cathy. "Almost as if it were your wedding instead of mine."

"Well, it might be soon," confessed the other.

Cathy jumped up to hug her. "Dr. Nairn? I suspected it the minute I told him you had broken off with Charles."

"So it was you he got the news from. Thank you, Cathy."

"As if you couldn't have told him yourself! Anyhow, I'm glad. It was worrying me that you couldn't be as happy as I am. Now everything is going to be perfect. Another cup to celebrate and one of those luscious cream cakes?"

"I ought not," said Hilda. "Dieting, you know," but she took one just the same.

From there they got on to the subject of clothes. Cathy's dress, ready and waiting, was a simple long frock of pale blue and white with a floppy hat to match.

As for Hilda, she had opted for an ensemble in rose pink with short jacket and long skirt. They chatted happily, their last long time together before the great day.

"I'm sorry you'll be leaving Nethershaw, Hilda, but think what fun it will be to visit each other. I'll keep you up to date on the happenings in this town, never fear!" She added, more soberly, "Goodness knows what is going to happen about Grandma Drummond."

"She hasn't come back, Cathy?"

"No, nor likely to. Yet I'm sure she's miserable. She won't be coming to the wedding either, Hilda. What I would give to see her sitting in the church pew beside the others!"

Hilda asked—"Have you really tried to persuade her?"

"Me? I wouldn't dare. She really hates me, I think. Neil and his father say she ought to be left alone to 'stew in her own juice,' as Susan Brodie puts it."

Hilda pondered. "All the same, I think you should have a go at it, Cathy. I'm sure you have great powers of persuasion."

"Not as regards Grandma Drummond! I'm scared of her, Hilda, and yet I would love Neil and her to be friends again. They're really very fond of each other. If it hadn't been for me—"

"Now, don't blame yourself. Mrs. Drummond is the one at fault. She should be grateful to Neil for bringing a girl like you into the family. I'd love to tell her so."

"Thanks, Hilda, but you might get more than you bargained for. Still, I'm sorry for the old soul."

"It's what you call cutting off your nose to spite your face." Hilda looked at the time—"Oh dear, I'll have to go. I'm due to meet David very soon."

"David? Oh yes, of course," laughed Cathy. "I forgot he had a first name."

They parted at the door, going their separate ways. Cathy's lay in the direction of the Greenview Home whose windows overlooked the street. Glancing across, she could see some of the residents gazing out with lack luster eyes. Time must go very slowly for them!

Grandma Drummond was not among them, however. She must be keeping herself to herself. Without visitors, what kind of life was she leading? You would think she'd be glad to see someone from outside, even someone she disapproved of.

Cathy stopped short. Now was her chance. Neil and his father might deem it useless, but she would make another attempt. All her life she had tried hard to be on good terms with people. As for her stepmother, she had at last won the day. She would go in there and speak peace, whatever the consequences.

She rang the bell and a small, harassed maid came to the door.

"I've come to see Mrs. Drummond. Can you tell me which room—?"

The girl replied, "Room seven, Miss, upstairs." Presumably she had not been told about the ban on visitors.

"She is quite well?" asked Cathy.

"Oh aye, Miss. She won't mix, that's all. Has her meals sent up to her."

"Right. I'll find my way." She was upstairs in a flash, knocking at the door.

"All right, come in!" came a peevish voice.

She opened the door and entered. The old lady was seated at a table on which was set a tray with cup and saucer. She had her back to her and did not turn. Her shoulders were sagging, her posture listless and uncaring.

"This tea," she complained, "is far too wishy-washy. Tell them that if I can't get some decent tea, I'll do without!"

Cathy moved across to her, but she still did not turn round.

The girl's hand went out to take the cup of weak, almost cold tea.

"I'll get you another cup."

At last she recognized her. "You! What are you doing here?"

"I came to see you. Oh, I know you didn't want anyone, but I was passing."

"Indeed. Why didn't you pass, then?"

Smiling, Cathy put a hand on her shoulder. "Because you were on my conscience."

"Huh . . . Don't tell me that. Young folk haven't got consciences nowadays."

"Oh, but they have, Gran! It makes me feel bad to think that, but for me, you'd still have been in your rightful place in Airlie House. Isn't that true?"

"Ay, it's true enough, but Airlie House for all its size, isn't big enough to hold the likes of you and me. So I'm not coming back, thank you."

"Well, at least you'll come to the wedding? It

won't be the same without you. Think it over, while I bring that cup of tea."

She found the kitchen, but there was no one there. Undeterred, she set about infusing a good strong brew, poured it, and carried it upstairs.

"There, it's nice and hot. Try it out for sugar."

Gran stirred and sipped. "The best cup I've had since I came here. It's a wonder they made it for you."

"They didn't," laughed Cathy. "I made it myself."

"You did?" For the first time she gave her a look of near approval. "At least you've got enterprise."

Cathy sat down beside her. "Gran, Neil's father has made it up with Aunt Jessie."

"Oh, he has, has he? She'll be at the wedding, I suppose. All the more reason why I should stay away."

"All the more reason why you shouldn't. It would make Neil very happy if you were to come, Gran!"

"Ach, Neil. I'm finished with him. He's been neglecting me," she complained.

"He took you at your word, about visiting, but he truly wants to be friends," said Cathy earnestly. "Do come, Gran! Make it a real, united family affair. You know what it says in the Bible—'If a house be divided against itself, that house cannot stand.' "

The old lady gave her a thoughtful look. "So, you know your Bible."

"I was brought up on it."

"It says quite a lot for your parents, then. Have you still got them?"

It was the first sign of interest she had taken in Cathy's family.

"Just my father. He's coming to the wedding. Come, too, and meet him."

She took the thin, wrinkled hand in hers, pleadingly—"Please, Gran!"

The other sat for awhile, brooding. Then she said uncertainly—

"Well, I might. But just 'might,' mind! Don't count on it."

Cathy's sunny smile flashed out. "Thank you, Gran! I'm so glad I popped in to see you," and she pressed a kiss on the parchment cheek.

Obeying her instinct had paid off. Whether Gran came to the wedding or not, she felt a link had been made between them.

The day came at last. Aunt Jessie appeared at Cathy's bedside with breakfast on a tray. Her niece sat up sharply.

"But why, Auntie—? I'm not ill."

"No, but I'm spoiling you for once. Take it, honey. It's not every day you get married."

She took it obediently, though excitement was mounting. From then on, everything went with a rush. Aunt Jessie kept phoning here, there, and everywhere, with sorties downstairs to the shop, which was being looked after today by a neighbor who, though obliging, was a bit slow.

Neil rang from Airlie House to ask if everything was all right and to say that his best man, a friend from college, had arrived in good trim and was Cathy feeling nervous because he was?

"Not a bit," she replied. "Poor Neil, I know men hate this sort of thing. You wish it was all over, don't you?"

"Yes, sweetheart. I can't wait to have you all to myself without all those people butting in. Thanks for understanding!"

Though she too could hardly wait for the minute when they would be alone together, she felt she must savor every second of this momentous day, the highlight of her life. To-morrow they would be traveling north to honeymoon near Kilgower. Tonight, this special night, would be spent in their own flat. It was the way Cathy wanted it.

Hilda appeared early on, looking handsome and regal in her bridesmaid's outfit. She was no longer depressed by the thought of being three times a bridesmaid, never a bride.

"I wasn't sure it was going to come true for me, Cathy! But now—"

"Your David came along. I'm so glad he'll be at the wedding! I have hopes of Grandmamma Drummond coming too, but she's quite unpre-dictable. Neil's parents are sure she won't be there, for she's never been known to shift her stand once she's taken it. However, they don't know about my attempts at persuasion. I've kept them secret, even from Neil."

While Hilda was helping her dress, Aunt Jessie kept popping in to report latest devel-opments. She had been disappointed that her niece had not chosen full bridal array with a long train and veil with orange blossom, but there you were, the modern girl had no respect for tradition. However, no bride could have looked bonnier than Cathy, whatever she wore.

Dr. Paton was of the same opinion. He turned up later with his wife to share with them a "put past" to keep them going until the wedding lunch. Then came the restless waiting until it was time to set off.

Things were happening in Airlie House, too. Susan Brodie, who was in charge there, kept them all on their toes. Being a romantic at heart, she knew everything there was to know about weddings. Though she and old Mrs. Drummond had never seen eye to eye, she was genuinely vexed about the old lady's departure, mainly for Neil's sake.

Neil himself had little hope of Gran relenting enough to come to the wedding. Such a perverse old lady, missing what should have been an event to sweeten her old age!

At noon, the wedding bells pealed out from the church tower. Besides the invited guests, it looked as if the whole population had rallied at the gate to greet the bride. Cathy waved to them as she passed through with her father, and they responded with a cheer.

In the church the organ was playing "Here Comes the Bride." Walking up the aisle on her father's arm, she saw that Neil was there waiting for her, and that was about all she saw until the wedding ceremony had passed in a happy blur.

Not until then did she feel free to look about

her. Her first glance, as she came back down the aisle with her new husband, was toward the front pews. What she saw put the final touch to her state of euphoria.

There, alongside Neil's relations, in a smart new hat trimmed with a white rose, sat Grandma Drummond. Stiff and formidable she still looked, but she was there!

Neil also had spied her. "Was it you who worked the miracle?" he asked his bride. She twinkled back at him. "I'll tell you later."

The lunch and reception over, the happy pair went back to Airlie House to calm down over a cup of tea with Neil's parents. Grandmamma was there too, her presence accepted as if she had never been away, except that she insisted she was going back to Greenview tonight. They did not try to dissuade her. She would go her own way whatever they said.

"Very well, Gran. I'll run you back when you're ready," Neil promised.

At last he and Cathy escaped to their own domain, their very own, with everything shining new and welcoming. He crushed her in his arms.

"Mine at last. You don't belong to those others, darling, you belong to me!"

She replied, her eyes shining, "I belong to myself, dear, but I want to share my life with you."

It was Cathy who reminded him, later, of his promise to take his grandmother back to Greenview.

Neil said, "Bother! I don't want to leave you."

"Nor do I want you to go. But it won't take long. And when you come back, Neil, I'll be waiting—"

He hurried off in order to get back all the more quickly.

Gran was looking tired, her head nodding.

"Ready to go?" he asked. "I'll take you along now."

She sat still. Then, glancing at her son, Andrew, and his wife, she inquired,

"Is there still an electric blanket on my bed, upstairs?"

"There is indeed," replied Evelyn. "I instructed Susan to switch it on an hour ago."

"But I told you I wasn't staying."

"I know, but just in case—"

Gran made to rise. "Give me my stick, Neil. Now you can help me upstairs."

Neil grinned over her head to his parents and got an answering wink from his father. Good. Dad was really on the road to recovery! Opening his grandmother's door, he saw that everything had been prepared. The electric heater was on and her night clothes laid out on the bed.

Gran sniffed a little and wiped her eyes, sinking on to her chair as if she had no more strength.

"I'm tired," she said. "Old age has beaten me. I can't fight any longer."

"You don't need to fight. Just sit back and enjoy life for a change! You weren't enjoying it in that rest home, were you?"

"Yon place," she declared, "was not a home. You couldn't even get a decent cup of tea! This is home. You're a good lad, Neil, and I believe you've chosen the right wife after all. She's got spunk, that lass!"

He was delighted. "You and Cathy are going to be great friends, I know. Before I leave you, Gran, here is a present for you. It was Cathy who thought of it."

So saying, he laid the magnificent Scrabble board on her knee.

"Neil!" she scolded. "You must have paid a fortune for this. It's a deluxe model, far too good!"

"Not for you," he assured her. "May I have a game with you, now and again?"

Dabbing at her eyes angrily, Gran replied, "Oh well, I suppose so. You might as well bring Cathy, too. I'd like to pit my wits against the pair of you!"

It was the final acceptance. Neil bent down to kiss her goodnight. Then, treading on air, he went hurrying back to his wife.